"Then why do I want you to kiss me again? I mean, I know all of the reasons why we shouldn't. That doesn't change anything though, does it? I still want you to kiss me."

Carrie hesitated then smiled. "You're soaking wet. Let me get you a towel."

Jill grabbed her arm as Carrie turned. "You want to just avoid it? You kiss me then you want to pretend it didn't happen?"

"I can't pretend it didn't happen, Jill. I've thought of little else since then. But if I don't leave and do something—like get you a towel—then I'm going to kiss you again. And then we will definitely have a problem."

It was an out. Jill could let her go, could let her escape into the cottage. They could avoid the subject, they could even have lunch. But Jill's grip tightened on Carrie's arm. She didn't want to let her go.

"Kiss me again," she whispered.

But Carrie shook her head. "No. No, I won't be the one." She stepped away, arms at her sides.

"I want . . . I want you to kiss me," Jill said again.

Carrie tilted her head, her eyes looking into Jill's very soul. "Then come kiss me," she whispered.

It was a command Jill couldn't resist. She took a step closer, feeling the electricity in the room, seeing the anticipation in Carrie's eyes. She was surprised at the pulse that beat rapidly at Carrie's throat, surprised at the difficulty she had breathing, surprised at the *need* she had to kiss Carrie.

Visit

Bella Books

at

BellaBooks.com

or call our toll-free number

1-800-729-4992

The
COTTAGE

Gerri Hill

Bella
BOOKS
2007

Bella Books, Inc.
P.O. Box 10543
Tallahassee, FL 32302

Printed in the United States of America on acid-free paper
First Edition

Editor: Anna Chinappi
Cover designer: LA Callaghan

ISBN-10: 1-59493-096-1
ISBN-13: 978-1-59493-096-6

To Diane . . . who's taught me to believe that all things are possible.

Acknowledgments

I would like to thank my good friend Jennifer Rudolph for her help in shaping the men in this book. Also, thanks again to Judy Underwood for her valuable feedback. A special thank you to my editor, Anna Chinappi, who has been a great pleasure to work with these past few years.

About the Author

Gerri Hill has nine published works, including Lambda finalists *Gulf Breeze* and *Artist's Dream*, and GCLS finalist *Hunter's Way*. She began writing lesbian romance as a way to amuse herself while snowed in one winter in the mountains of Colorado and hasn't looked back. Her first published work came in 2000 with *One Summer Night*. Hill's love of nature and being outdoors usually makes its way into her stories as her characters often find themselves in beautiful natural settings. When she isn't writing, Hill and her longtime partner, Diane, can be found at their home in East Texas, where their vegetable garden, orchard and five acres of woods keep them busy. They share their lives with two labs, Max and Zach, and an assortment of furry felines. For more, see her Web site at www.gerrihill.com.

CHAPTER ONE

She wiped the tears from her eyes, telling herself over and over that it was just a memorial service. They weren't really burying her. Not really.

But the sobs came again and she stumbled, one hand reaching out to steady herself, the other covering her mouth as she tried to keep her emotions in check.

"Miss? Are you all right?"

Jill turned, startled. She hadn't seen anyone else. The others—the family—were all at the grave site. She stared at the elderly woman, embarrassed by her lack of control. She shook her head slowly then fumbled in her purse for another tissue.

"Are you a friend of the family, dear?"

Jill cleared her throat, her voice hoarse from crying. "Excuse me. But what?"

"She was so young. You were close?"

Jill nodded then blew her nose.

"I didn't know the family. They rarely went to church," the woman said with just a hint of disapproval in her voice. "But my niece works at one of his stores."

"I see." Jill dabbed at her eyes, cursing herself for coming. She knew it would serve no purpose. She'd already said her good-byes. But no, she had to come. She wanted to see *them*. And it only served to accentuate her breakdown. A breakdown in front of a perfect stranger.

"I come to visit my Eddie nearly every day. He's been gone three years now."

Jill frowned, turned and stared at the monument she was leaning against. Edward Jorkowski.

"Oh my God," Jill murmured. "I'm so sorry."

"Oh, I doubt Eddie minds. He probably enjoys the company." The woman patted the seat next to her on the bench. "Come, sit with me a bit. Tell me about your friend there. People are always afraid to talk about the dead, as if they didn't exist. My own kids, my grandkids, after Eddie died, they hardly ever mentioned him. As if they thought he wasn't always on my mind anyway."

"You were married a long time?"

"Oh, yes. Sixty-three years. A long time to be with someone. A long time to love someone. People don't realize the huge void in one's life after a death. Oh, people say, I know how you feel but they really don't. Not unless they've lost someone too."

"I suppose you're right."

"Come, sit with me for awhile."

Jill was about to decline. She hadn't told *anyone* about her. About *them*. About their life. But the old woman's skin crinkled as she smiled, her brown eyes warm and inviting.

Jill sighed and cleared her throat. "The funeral was private. Family only. The service out here was private too."

"Oh. So you're crashing it?"

Jill smiled sadly, nodding. "Yeah. She was . . . she was cremated." Jill motioned with her hand. "Who has a service in the cemetery when they're not even burying them?"

The woman shrugged. "I guess they're going to put a headstone down, give her kids someplace to go to." The woman patted the bench again. "Come sit. My name is Beatrice. My Eddie always called me Bea."

Jill smiled. "Bea. I'm Jill."

"I never understood private funerals. I mean, there's more than just the family who wants to say good-bye. Like you, for instance."

Jill sat down heavily on the bench, her eyes sliding back to the family as they stood holding hands. The pastor was speaking, his hands outstretched to the sky. Jill shook her head. God, she would have hated this.

"They didn't know I existed. Still don't. But I loved her so," Jill whispered. "And she loved me."

"I don't understand."

Jill swallowed and cleared her throat again. "We met by chance less than a year ago." Jill turned, facing Bea. "Do you believe in soul mates?"

CHAPTER TWO

A year earlier

It was a glorious January day and Jill found a quiet park bench. *Her* park bench. She slid to one side—the end still in bright sunshine—and unwrapped the sandwich she'd made that morning. She'd been coming to the park for years, enjoying the lake and woods while she escaped from the city for an hour each day. Development on the north side of the lake had the city streets encroaching on the park but the quiet remained. The lake and surrounding woods totaled over a thousand acres, land that local developers had been salivating over for years. And little by little, the county would sell a few acres here and there, shrinking the park while developers kept the county commissioners' pockets lined with cash. Jill was proud to have served on the Citizens Action Committee which helped pass a ballot initiative to stop any future land sales.

"Bunch of idiot politicians," she murmured.

But the park was safe now. No matter how much the city grew—and it seemed it was getting bigger each year—this land would be here, undisturbed.

She bit into her sandwich, scanning the picnic area, seeing familiar faces but none of whom she knew. They were just faces of people like her, coming to the park for a quick escape. She never felt the urge to talk to any of them, but people-watching had become a hobby.

And then she saw her. The painter. The woman had been here every day for the last two weeks. She was closer today, standing out at the edge of the trees, facing the lake. She didn't have an easel this time, just a large sketchpad. As Jill watched her, the woman leaned back against the tree, head cocked sideways as she studied the lake.

Jill wondered who she was and where she was from. Her salt-and-pepper hair hinted at her age, that and the reading glasses that were sometimes perched on top of her head. But her lithe, graceful body contradicted those signs of an older woman. Jill stared, transfixed as her hand moved across the paper. She had a nearly overwhelming urge to walk closer, just to see what the woman was sketching. The lake, most likely, but still, Jill had to see.

Something was pulling her, urging her up off the park bench. Surprised, she found herself creeping closer to the woman, peering over her shoulder. She saw the woman's hand still, then watched as she slowly turned, sensing her presence. She slid the tiny reading glasses back to the more familiar position on top of her head. In the brief seconds that their eyes met, Jill noticed two things. One, her salt-and-pepper hair did indeed belie her age. She couldn't have been much older than Jill. And two, there was something so familiar about her, she nearly stopped breathing. Pale blue eyes collided with her own and a warm smile transformed the woman's face.

"Hi."

Jill finally remembered to breathe. She smiled in return, a bit apologetically. "I'm sorry but curiosity got the better of me," she explained.

"Oh, my sketch." The woman held out the pad. "Here, take a look."

Jill gasped then looked up, again meeting pale blue eyes. "It's . . . it's me. Sort of."

The woman laughed. "Yeah, sort of. I've seen you on that same bench for days. I thought I would try and sketch it from memory. I didn't want to actually sit and stare at you. That freaks some people out."

Jill laughed too and handed the pad back. "And here I thought I was observing you in secret."

"No, people are generally curious when they see someone painting out in public. Or sketching, as is the case today." The woman held out her hand. "I'm Carrie Howell, by the way."

Jill took her hand, noting how strong the slim fingers were that wrapped around her own. "Jill. Jill Richardson."

"Nice to meet you, Jill. You come out here often?"

Jill nodded. "Nearly everyday. When the weather's good."

"Lunch break?"

"Yes, one to two."

Carrie nodded. "I usually come around one myself. It's too crowded during the noon hour, especially on gorgeous days like today." She pointed to the lake. "I was actually hoping someone would take a paddleboat or canoe out. I love sketching the lake when it's calm like this."

"But you do more than sketch. I saw you with an easel the other day."

"I use mostly chalk or charcoal if I'm not painting with watercolors. That's my favorite. And on the few occasions I feel daring, I play with acrylic or oils but not often." She shrugged. "It's just a hobby, really. I could always sketch but I've taken classes for watercolors and other mediums."

"Well, nice hobby to have. It must be relaxing." Jill motioned back to her park bench. "But I'm cutting into your time. I'll let you get back to it."

"Maybe it's me who is cutting into your time," Carrie said with a laugh. "It was nice to meet you, Jill. Thanks for being the subject for my sketch."

"Any time."

Jill walked back to her bench, her sandwich long forgotten. She couldn't shake the feeling that their meeting was somehow preordained. Although she knew she'd never met Carrie Howell before, the familiarity of her eyes indicated otherwise. Jill would swear she'd stared into them before.

As she drove back to her tiny office on Oak Street, she replayed her meeting with Carrie, trying in vain to recall a time when she may have possibly run into the woman before. Nothing would come to her, so she simply attributed it to one of those déjà vu feelings you could never explain.

But she felt certain she would see Carrie Howell again.

CHAPTER THREE

Jill drove into her driveway at exactly five twenty, the same time she got home every day. Their modest home was in an older neighborhood, the huge trees indicating the age of most of the houses. Some of the older homes had been torn down and replaced with newer, upscale versions but the trees remained. She and Craig had bought the home shortly after they'd married. His parents had been kind enough to give them the down payment. *Right.* She knew now that it had simply been their way of controlling them. She and Craig, both just out of college, both teaching at the same high school, had hardly had the funds for a house. But his parents found just the perfect house for them. And as an added bonus, it wasn't even a block from their own.

Jill rolled her eyes, wondering why she'd allowed it in the first place. But the truth was, she'd fallen in love with the two-story house, the big trees, the huge yard, the quiet neighborhood. So it seemed a blessing at the time when they offered the down payment. She just had no idea they'd be involved in their life as much as they were.

She parked her car in the driveway well to the right to give Craig room to pull in his truck. The two-car garage was packed, with room for only one vehicle. Craig's new truck meant Jill had to park her old Subaru outside now. It had seen some years but she couldn't bear to part with it, not when gas prices were what they were and she was getting well over thirty miles to the gallon. She raised a corner of her mouth in a smile and raised her eyebrows. But it wasn't like she went anywhere. Back and forth to work, back and forth to town, hauling Angie around. She hadn't taken a real trip in years. In fact, they'd not even gone on a vacation since Angie was ten. The older Angie grew, the more activities she seemed to be involved in. Activities that took up most of the summer.

She was barely in the kitchen door when her daughter ran into the room, a scowl on her face as she placed both hands on her hips. It was a gesture Jill used to find amusing, knowing Angie had picked it up from her over the years, but now it was simply annoying.

"Do you have any idea what time it is?"

"Yes, I know exactly what time it is. It's the same time I get home every day."

"Mom, I had a study group meeting at Shelly's house. We have a biology project we're working on."

"Why didn't you ask your grandmother to take you?" Jill asked as she opened the fridge and pulled out a bottle of water, absently wondering what she'd fix for dinner tonight.

"Grandma always has to take me places. Why can't you take me?"

"I work until five every day, Angie, you know that. If you need to be somewhere before then, ask your grandmother. You're at her house after school anyway."

"She shouldn't have to take me all the time. She's not my mother."

Jill closed her eyes for a moment. Apparently her mother-in-law was in one of her moods. It was on those occasions she preached to Angie how terrible it was that Jill didn't teach school anymore, how horrible it was that she had to work until five, well past the time her only child was home from school.

But Jill would not argue with her fourteen-year-old daughter.

"Okay, let's go," she said.

"Go where?"

"To your study group."

"It's too late now, Mom."

"Then why are we having this conversation?"

"You just don't get it, do you?"

"Apparently not," she murmured. "Where's your father?"

"He's got a game tonight."

"Oh, yeah, I forgot. Do you know when he'll be home?"

"He's your husband, not mine."

Jill stared as her daughter walked out of the kitchen in the same huff she'd walked in. Four more years of high school. *Wonder if I can rent her out until she graduates?*

"Probably not."

She'd been in this kind of mood for the last six months, since she'd started high school. It was like someone flipped a switch. Her happy-go-lucky daughter had turned into the bitch from hell. And she knew her mother-in-law just egged her on, pointing out all of Jill's failings as a mother. One being the fact that she quit the teaching job all those years ago, a job which would have afforded her the opportunity to spend quality time with her daughter each summer. The truth was, Jill quit teaching because she couldn't stand being around teenagers when their hormones played havoc with their personalities. She was afraid she'd never want to have children of her own after spending her days with them. So, after only four years, she quit. She found a job as office manager for Tutt Construction shortly thereafter and she'd been with them ever since. When old Mr. Tutt handed the business over to his son eight years ago, Jill suddenly found herself with a nice raise and a new assistant. Seems Johnny knew her worth and all she did, even though his father had treated her—and paid her—as an entry level secretary. Jill kept the accounts organized, kept everyone on schedule and handled all the advertising.

And now that she had an assistant, it was a relatively stress-free job that she left at five each day and rarely thought of again until she arrived at eight the next morning. No, her only stress now was a teenage daughter whose hormones had attacked her from within and who got immense pleasure out of driving her mother insane.

It'll pass. Words Craig had used just the other night. The problem was, Craig was hardly home so he didn't notice the change in Angie. Unlike Jill, Craig loved teaching high school. It kept him young, he said. It also kept him away from the house. Football in the fall, basketball in the winter, baseball in spring, Craig coached them all. And in the summers, he played on no less than three softball teams. On his off nights, he volunteered his time at the little league fields.

It was no wonder they'd only had one child.

She took a package of ground beef from the freezer, wishing she could remember where his game was tonight and if he'd be home at a reasonable hour. Out-of-town games would get him home at eleven or later. If the game was at the gym, he'd be home by nine thirty. She'd make up a casserole. If he was hungry when he got home, at least she'd have something. If not, then tomorrow's dinner was already prepared.

She sighed, wondering when her marriage had evolved into this, wondering if all marriages got this way after nearly twenty years. They rarely talked. Hell, they rarely saw each other. Their sex life had become the obligatory once-a-week whether they wanted to or not. That was once a week on a good week. More often than not, Jill was in bed and asleep when Craig made it home. And that was another issue with her mother-in-law—Jill should be out supporting Craig, going to his games. After all, that's what the other wives did.

Which was bullshit, of course. And Craig didn't expect her to travel to games, just to watch him coach. It was ridiculous. However, he did want her to attend his summer softball games. And she did on occasion. She knew most of the other wives and got on well with them. But it got old, sitting for hours, watching a bunch of grown men acting like teenagers, each trying to outdo the other and show off their softball prowess.

Changing out of her business clothes, she slipped on a comfortable pair of sweats and an old baggy shirt of Craig's. As she robotically began preparing dinner, she poured a glass of wine, something she'd been indulging in for the last year or so. Neither she nor Craig were big drinkers, although he did enjoy an occasional beer with his softball buddies. But she'd bought a bottle of red wine on a whim one day and enjoyed having a glass with dinner. Dinner that she most often ate alone or with Angie. Lately, she'd begun enjoying a glass during the preparation of dinner too.

As she systematically added onions to the beef, she thought of the woman she'd met that day. Again, that nagging feeling of familiarity crept over her. She leaned a hip against the counter as she added more wine to her glass, wondering if she'd see her again tomorrow.

CHAPTER FOUR

Jill waved to her assistant at noon as the younger woman left for lunch. Jill always enjoyed the quiet in the office from noon until one. The phone rarely rang, giving her time to concentrate on the books. Accounting was a skill she had to forcibly learn when she took this job. Surprisingly, she found she was very good at it, intuitively so. But she hated interruptions. And now that she had an assistant to take care of the mundane chores around the small office, she could afford to close her door, shutting herself off while she balanced the accounts.

But now during lunch, her door was wide open on the off chance a customer might come in while Harriet was gone. Their business was still relatively small but had grown considerably since Johnny had taken over. He was more hands-on than his father had been, beating them to the office each morning, then leaving at nine to check on the various construction crews he had out in the field. Whereas his father ran the office and relied on his crews to run the construction end of things, Johnny allowed Jill to run the office while he managed the crews. It had been a profitable change for the business. A change that kept them all busy from eight to five.

But now Jill found herself watching the clock, wishing for one p.m. to arrive. She was anxious for her own lunch hour, anxious to go to the park. For some reason, she couldn't get Carrie Howell out of her mind. Even this morning, after Angie had thrown a fit about Jill not being able to take her to band practice at four, she longed for the quiet hour when she could escape to the park. God forbid Angie should hang around school for forty-five minutes until practice started.

"Mom, that's for losers. Those without a ride."

"Well, it looks like you'll be a loser today. Unless your grand-mother can take you."

"Of course, push your motherly duties off on Grandma," she said sarcastically.

"My motherly duties right now include working from eight to five. I don't have the luxury of being home all day like your grandmother."

"I can't wait until I'm old enough to drive. Then I won't have to rely on you anymore," she spat.

"Your grandmother's going to buy you a car, is she?"

"Dad promised I could have a car," she yelled.

"Yes. I think he promised you my old Subaru."

Tears welled up immediately. "I'm not driving that piece of crap! I'll be laughed out of high school."

She ran screaming from the room and Jill rubbed her temples, wishing once again that Craig was here to witness one of her little fits.

And after a completely silent trip to school, one that ended with Angie slamming the door on the Subaru, Jill escaped to the quiet and calm of her eight-to-five job.

She looked again at the clock, watching the hands move to twelve thirty, knowing she was getting absolutely no work done as she listened to the ticking of the clock.

Finally, with only five minutes to go, she began getting ready, saving the little work she'd done, closing down her computer. She walked to the tiny break room and retrieved her sandwich from the refrigerator, then grabbed a plastic bottle of water and waited patiently at her desk. As soon as she saw Harriet drive up, she rushed to the door, meeting her on the sidewalk.

"You're in a hurry today," Harriet said. "Got a date?"

Jill laughed. "A date with a park bench, yes."

"Well have fun. See you at two."

Yes, she was in a hurry today and the morning had been endless. And the anticipation she'd been feeling all day manifested itself tenfold as she approached the park. She didn't pause to wonder why she was in such a hurry to get to the park, in such a hurry to see if Carrie Howell was there today. Again, that feeling that she was being controlled in some way, being guided to the park, settled over her and she knew it would be futile to try to challenge it. She didn't want to challenge it.

She wanted to see Carrie Howell.

And as she eased onto her park bench, letting the sun warm her, she looked around, her eyes searching for the other woman. A moment of panic hit when she didn't see her on first glance, then through the trees, near the lake, she stood. Easel again today.

Jill felt a wave of relief wash over her at the sight of the other woman. She couldn't explain the comfort she felt, knowing Carrie was here. Without thought, she unwrapped her sandwich, eating and chewing methodically as she watched Carrie.

Then, as if sensing her eyes on her, Carrie turned and stared right at her. Jill stopped chewing, her throat tight as she imagined those pale blue eyes looking at her. Carrie lifted a hand in greeting and Jill did the same. It wasn't until Carrie turned back around that Jill was able to swallow again.

What is wrong with you?

But she had no answer. She simply had an overwhelming urge to be near the woman. And before long, she would get her wish as Carrie walked toward her. Jill hastily wiped her mouth with her napkin and took a swallow of water.

"Hi, Jill. Good to see you again," Carrie greeted.

"Yes. I see you have your easel today. Watercolors?"

"No. Colored chalk. I usually just use my sketch pad but I had an inspiration for a larger picture. I wanted to capture the trees and lake, maybe add a duck or two in the foreground. If it turns out good with the colored chalk, then I'll do the scene with watercolors." Then she opened her notebook and handed Jill a paper. "Here. Thought you might want to have this."

Jill took the paper, noting the sketch she'd seen yesterday, the sketch of her on the park bench. Carrie had added features to her face, making it obvious it was her, not just a faceless woman in the park. It was beautiful.

"Thank you. It's lovely."

"Well, I had a lovely subject."

Jill smiled, not knowing what to say.

Out of her bag, Carrie pulled a half a loaf of bread. "I was about to go feed the ducks. Feel like walking along?"

"Sure." Jill stood, motioning to the easel. "Will that be okay?"

"I doubt anyone will swipe it," Carrie said.

They walked along the trail, heading to the small piers where paddleboats and canoes were tied. In spring and summer, you'd be hard-pressed to find one available as the lake would be littered with them. But today, on this cool January afternoon, no one had braved the water.

"I can't decide which time of year is my favorite out here," Carrie said. "I like the quiet of winter, like today. But I miss the greenness of spring and summer. When I sketch in the winter, I

16

try to find something bright, something colorful. Like one of the red canoes on the water, for instance."

"I've never seen you here before but I take it you're familiar with the lake," Jill said.

"I'm familiar with the lake, yes. I don't often come here to the park, though. Especially during the summer. Way too many kids running around," she said. "Not that I have anything against kids. They're just . . . disturbing," Carrie said with a laugh.

"Yes, I'll have to agree."

Carrie laughed. "Let me guess. You have a teenager."

Jill nodded. "A daughter."

"Oh, my."

"She's fourteen, thinks she's eighteen and acts like ten. Do you have kids?"

Carrie nodded. "Two boys. Josh is seventeen and will graduate in May. Aaron is fifteen. Couldn't ask for better kids. Josh has always been mature for his age, and thankfully, they get along well. Josh actually enjoys being taxi service for Aaron, so that saves me right there. He's taken his role of big brother very seriously."

"Angie is at the I Hate My Mother stage," Jill explained.

"It's a girl thing," Carrie said. "My mother reminds me I was at that stage for fifteen years," she said with a laugh.

They approached the swim area, deserted this time of year except for the ducks that were sunning themselves on the sand. As if sensing a free lunch, no less than ten came over to meet them. Carrie handed Jill several slices of bread and they went about the fun chore of tearing it up and tossing it to the clamoring ducks at their feet.

"Oh, here she comes," Carrie said, pointing to a late arrival. "I call her Grandma Duck."

"Is she old?"

Carrie shrugged. "I have no idea. But she's more gray than brown, and see how she limps." Carrie squatted down. "Here, sweetie," she murmured, tossing bread to the old duck.

Jill watched, smiling as Carrie shooed the other ducks aside so Grandma Duck could eat.

"I've seen her around for years," Carrie said. "She's a tough old broad."

The loaf of bread was devoured quickly, so they made their way back to the park bench. It was a fun hour but it passed far too quickly.

"Can I ask you something?"

Carrie nodded. "Sure."

"Have we met before?"

Carrie laughed. "You too? I've been thinking about it since yesterday. You seem so familiar to me."

"I know. But I don't think we've met." Jill allowed her eyes to linger on Carrie's pale blue ones. "Surely we would remember."

Carrie's eyes turned serious. "Perhaps in another life," she murmured.

Jill was about to say she didn't believe in that sort of thing but the familiarity in Carrie's eyes told her it might be true. "Perhaps."

Carrie smiled, her eyes softening. "And perhaps I'll see you again."

CHAPTER FIVE

Jill was surprised to see Craig's truck in the driveway when she got home that afternoon. She knew he didn't have a game but they usually practiced after school. She noticed two things when she walked into the kitchen. One, dinner was in the oven. He'd apparently found the casserole she'd made the night before. And two, the washer and dryer were both running.

"Craig?" she called.

"In here."

She found him in his recliner, the remote control in one hand and his cell phone in the other. A basketball game was on.

"Thanks for starting dinner," she said as she walked behind him, lightly squeezing his shoulder. "And laundry."

"How was your day?"

She smiled and shrugged. "Same as always." She rarely spoke about her job. On the few occasions she did try to share something with him, she could tell he was totally disinterested. If it didn't have to do with sports, his attention span was that of a ten-year-old. "You?"

"Short day. I blew off practice. We were awesome last night. I told them to take a day off."

"Well that was nice of you." She moved away. "Was Angie here? She had band practice."

"Yeah, I took her. She's going to catch a ride home."

"So I'm assuming she didn't give you grief like she did me this morning?"

Craig laughed. "The way I heard it, you gave her grief. My mother said Angie called her in tears."

Jill sighed. "And what else did your mother say?"

"Oh, the usual. By the way, we're invited to dinner Saturday night."

"Can't wait," she murmured as she left the room.

Alone in their bedroom, she undressed quickly, intending to take a shower before dinner. But Craig surprised her when he opened the door.

"We've got thirty minutes before Angie is home," he said, his eyebrows rising mischievously. He smiled, causing his moustache to crinkle at the corners.

But she closed her eyes and shook her head. "I'm not really in the mood, Craig," she said quietly.

He walked closer. "It's been a long time, babe."

"Yes, I know. It's been awhile since we've both actually been here at the same time."

"So? Is that a yes?"

Before she could answer, his cell rang. He looked at it, then back at Jill. "Sorry, babe, but I've got to take this."

She shook her head, surprised at the relief she felt as he closed the door behind him. No, she wasn't in the mood, but that hadn't stopped her before. But for some reason, this time she couldn't muster the energy to fake it.

And instead of the quick shower she'd planned, she filled the tub with water, adding scents and oils to the hot water. She lit the lone candle she kept there then turned the lights down. It was a romantic setting. So before she slipped into the warm water, she locked the bathroom door. Just in case.

She let the water envelope her, sinking down to her neck and closing her eyes. She wasn't surprised when thoughts of Carrie Howell danced in her mind.

CHAPTER SIX

"*That* Howell? The electronics store?" Jill asked a few days later as they walked to feed the ducks.

"Yes, that Howell, but it's not that big a deal," Carrie said.

"Is that really your husband in the commercials?"

"That's really him."

"Wow. He's attractive."

Carrie shrugged. "He's getting the middle-age spread."

"How long have you been married?"

"Twenty-two years. We seldom see each other, though. I'm certain that's a requirement for a good marriage. You're never around each other enough to argue. But he's a workaholic. He has seven stores now. Two in town here and the rest within a two-hundred-mile radius. He's convinced he has to visit each one personally once a week."

"Wow."

"That impresses you?"

"Seven stores? Yeah, it does. How'd he get started?"

Carrie pointed. "There's Grandma Duck. She's waiting for us." She paused, her eyes still on the duck. "When we got married, James had every gadget known to man. CDs were just getting off the ground, computers were still in their infancy and cell phones were about this big," she said with a laugh, holding her hands apart. "But, if they made it, James had to have it." She handed Jill some bread then began tossing it to the ducks, making sure Grandma Duck got her share.

"So that prompted him to open his own store of gadgets?"

"Pretty much. That was before the days of the big chain stores. He made a decent living but when it became the norm for everyone to have a home computer, that's when his business really took off. That, and when everything went digital. Phones and cameras. He was way ahead of the game and he already had a reputation."

"So when the big stores moved in, it didn't cut into his business?"

"Some. But most of his other stores are in smaller towns where the competition is nearly nonexistent."

"So you don't work then?"

Carrie shook her head. "Not anymore. But it really didn't have anything to do with James. I was in real estate for years. I had my own money."

When Jill would have asked another question, Carrie turned to her, her blue eyes clear as they met Jill's.

"You have got to be bored silly hearing about my husband's ascent in the business world. Tell me what you do."

Again, that sense of familiarity settled over her as she looked into Carrie's eyes. She smiled before turning back to the ducks.

"I don't even tell my husband about my job, why in the world would you want to hear about it?"

"Because I'm interested in you."

It was a simple answer said with the casualness of a new friendship. But for some reason, the words echoed in her brain. Why in the world would Carrie Howell be interested in her?

"I manage an office," Jill finally said. "Tutt Construction. I've been there since I quit teaching, fifteen years now."

"Oh? You were a teacher? I always think of it as being the worst possible job on the planet," she said with a laugh. "I don't blame you for quitting. So what does one do to manage an office?"

"Well, there's the owner, Mr. Tutt's son Johnny who took over about eight years ago. There's my assistant, who now handles all of the really important things, like making sure there's coffee in the morning. That leaves me to juggle the accounts and keep them reconciled, deal with the accountants, deal with the bank and do payroll for the construction crews."

"You wear quite a few hats," Carrie said.

Jill shook her head. "I've been there so long, I could do it in my sleep," she said. "It's a relatively stress-free job that brings in more income than my husband's."

"Ouch. That must hurt," Carrie guessed.

"He's a teacher. And a coach," she added. "At Kline High."

"So you were both teachers? What prompted you to quit?"

"I realized I hated teenagers."

Carrie's laughter rang out, startling the ducks as they scurried away from them.

"And now you're living with one. That's priceless."

"Glad you find it amusing," Jill said with a smile.

CHAPTER SEVEN

The inane conversation over dinner was endless and Jill found it hard to keep an interested look on her face. She'd heard Craig's childhood stories more times than she could count—they all had—yet his mother continued, droning on and on until Jill felt her eyes rolling to the back of her head.

"Grandma, tell the one where Dad fell out of the tree," Angie coaxed.

"Oh, I remember when that happened," Craig's uncle chimed in.

Jill looked across the table at Craig, silently begging him to put an end to the storytelling. He gave her a subtle wink then turned his attention to his mother who had already begun the story.

Rude or not, Jill simply could not stand it another second. She stood, quietly pointing to the bathroom. Her mother-in-law never missed a beat.

She closed the door then turned on the water, letting the sound drown out the voices in the other room. She met her eyes in the mirror, wondering at her irritability this evening. Of course her in-laws got on her nerves—they always had—but she thought she'd be used to it by now. The once-a-month dinner party his parents hosted had become so routine, Jill hardly gave it a thought anymore. But tonight, she simply could not take another second of it. She sighed, then brushed at the blond hair covering her ears, then fluffed her bangs a bit. She sighed again.

The restlessness she'd felt all day seemed to escalate as she sat through dinner, growing with each word her mother-in-law uttered. As she stared into the mirror, she saw the truth in her hazel eyes and she knew why she felt restless. She didn't understand it, but she knew why.

It was Saturday.

And as her luck would have it, Monday proved to be a rainy day. She didn't care. She went to the park anyway.

It was empty.

So she sat in her car, her disappointment nearly choking her as she nibbled at her sandwich. No, she didn't understand it. How could she become obsessed with a woman she'd known but a week? What was it about Carrie Howell that drew her?

Lost in thought, she gasped at the urgent knocking on her window. She wiped at the fog on the glass, her smile matching that of Carrie's as the other woman stared back at her.

Jill quickly unlocked the doors, watching as Carrie hurried around to the passenger's door, pausing to close her umbrella before getting inside.

"Are you crazy?" Jill asked as the dripping woman got inside her car.

"Apparently. Sorry about your seat here."

"I doubt you could possibly do damage to this old car."

Jill watched as Carrie ran wet hands through her hair, brushing at the drops of water that clung to her short strands.

"I never told you this before, but I love your hair," Jill said without thinking.

"Thanks. I gave up coloring it about ten years ago. Runs in the family. My mother was totally gray by forty so I've got her beat. I still have a little pepper mixed in."

"How old are you?"

"Forty-three. You?"

"Still clinging to thirty-nine. For a few more months anyway."

"Well, we'll celebrate. Forty is a great year."

"I think you're the only woman I've ever heard say that." Jill smiled. "And what are you doing out here in the rain?"

"I could ask you the same question." Carrie's eyes softened as they looked at Jill. "But I imagine you're doing the same thing I am."

Jill nodded. "I . . . yes, I suppose I am."

"So, how was your weekend?"

"Endless."

"Funny. That's how I was going to describe mine."

"We had dinner at Craig's parents' house Saturday night. A family thing. Some of his out-of-town relatives showed up."

"You don't get along with the in-laws?"

"We tolerate each other. His mother has not forgiven me for quitting teaching. That's just one on a long list of shortcomings I have."

"Let me guess. Craig is an only child?"

"Right."

"Mothers-in-law can be brutal."

"Yours?"

Carrie smiled. "No, she's actually a sweetheart. I get along better with her than my own mother."

"I guess I was lucky in that regard. My mother and I rarely had arguments. And she's my saving grace now whenever Arlene pisses me off. But I don't get to see her much. She remarried after my father died. Now they spend their time traveling around in a motor home."

"Oh, how fun. Just imagine the freedom."

"Yeah. I miss seeing her but she's having a blast. I can't begrudge her for that."

A loud clap of thunder nearly shook the vehicle and the steady drizzle of earlier turned into a downpour. They looked at each other and smiled.

"You may be stuck in here," Jill said.

"Well, I could think of worse places to be stuck." She glanced at her watch. "But you only have twenty minutes left. I should have come earlier."

"Six minutes. That's how long it takes to drive back to the office. But it won't be the end of the world if I'm late."

"No, but I bet it would be shocking. I picture you as one of those very punctual types and it probably drives you crazy to be late somewhere."

Jill laughed. "And how do you know this?"

"Because you get to the park at exactly five after one each day and leave the park at exactly seven till two."

Jill laughed again. "It gives me a minute to spare."

"But you haven't finished your lunch," Carrie said, pointing to the half-eaten sandwich. "I shouldn't have barged in on you. I just took a chance you might be here."

"Actually, I was disappointed it was raining. I didn't think you'd be here. I mean, not that I expect you to entertain me during lunch or anything," she added quickly.

Carrie laughed. "I enjoy your company too. I don't have a lot of girlfriends anymore," she said. "It seems that once I retired from real estate, I just lost touch with most of them. James and I have couple friends but I don't really have any close friends all to myself."

"I know what you mean. Our friends are other coaches and their wives. Or his softball buddies and their wives."

"Funny how that is, isn't it."

"I'm not nearly as outgoing as he is," Jill explained. "I enjoy my alone time too much. Craig, on the other hand, has to have constant entertainment, either in person or on his cell. I swear, he sleeps with the damn thing."

"I've got one just like that. I can relate."

"You probably don't even have a cell phone, do you?"

Carrie laughed. "I was the one sleeping with it when I was working. I mean, I have one still but I rarely have it on unless I need to call someone. I don't like the interruptions."

They sat for a moment, both quiet. Jill knew she should be leaving and she glanced quickly at her watch.

"I know. You need to go."

Jill nodded slowly. "Yes. Time. But it's pouring. Can I drop you somewhere?"

"Oh, no. I love the rain, really. When it's over and the sun comes out, everything is all fresh and clean. I love it. Besides, I know the more rain we get now, the greener it'll be come spring." She smiled. "Colors, my dear. An artist's best friend."

"Well, maybe tomorrow—"

"We'll have sunshine," Carrie finished for her. She reached to the floorboard of the car and retrieved her wet umbrella. "Drive carefully, Jill."

Before Jill could reply, Carrie had slipped out into the rain. She was but a shadow through the foggy windows and Jill sat for a moment, watching her disappear into the trees.

CHAPTER EIGHT

"I can't believe you've never been in a canoe," Carrie said as they tossed bread to the ducks later that week.

"I've been in a paddleboat. Does that count?"

Carrie fixed her pale blue eyes on her, a slow smile forming. "When the weather warms, we'll rent one."

Jill nodded, then lifted her shoulders inside her jacket, trying to stay warm. "It's downright frigid today."

"And didn't your mother warn you about being outside without your head covered?"

Carrie took the wool cap off her own head and covered Jill's, pulling it down around her ears. She laughed then brushed Jill's hair out of her eyes.

"There."

Jill laughed, staring at Carrie's short hair, the salt-and-pepper strands standing in disarray. "Maybe you should keep it," she teased. "You might scare off the ducks."

"Funny girl. You know, I haven't seen you eat lunch all week. Am I cutting into your time?"

"And I haven't seen you sketch. Perhaps it's me cutting into *your* time."

"I can sketch anytime. I enjoy our visits too much to interrupt them."

"Do you?"

Carrie stopped and turned, her eyes serious. "Yes, of course. You've become the highlight of my days."

"God, if that's the case, you must have very boring days."

"Boring? No, not really. But I look forward to seeing you. It's funny, you know. I'd watched you for over a week, sitting on your park bench. And as a people-watcher, you try to guess who they are, what they are, what their life is like. But you, I couldn't quite nail it. You were doing your own people-watching too. You never brought a book to read, you just sat there and looked around. I always wondered what you were thinking." She tossed the last of the bread to the ducks then dusted off her hands on her jeans. "You seemed a bit unapproachable, so I had already decided I wouldn't interrupt your days. That didn't stop me from sketching you," she added with a laugh.

"Did I really seem unapproachable?"

"Well, let me ask you this. In all the time you've been coming here, has anyone ever just walked up to you and started a conversation?"

Jill frowned and shook her head. "No. I guess not."

"You probably didn't realize it but you always picked a spot that was away from others, away from the footpath and away from the lake." She shrugged. "Away from traffic. Away from people."

Jill smiled then slipped two fingers under the warm wool cap to scratch her ear. "You overanalyze, don't you?"

Carrie laughed, again scattering the ducks. Jill loved her

laugh, deep and rich. It echoed around them.

"You just say what's on your mind, don't you?"

"As do you."

Carrie nodded. "Yes, I tend to overanalyze. So, my depiction of you as hating people is not true?"

It was Jill's turn to laugh. "I don't hate people. It's just teenagers, remember."

"And mothers-in-law," Carrie added.

They retraced their steps, heading back to the park bench that Jill normally occupied. As usual, the hour had flown by. And tomorrow was another Friday.

"Do you have plans for the weekend?" Carrie asked.

Jill nodded. "Craig has an out-of-town basketball tournament on Saturday. I've promised to take Angie and a couple of her friends to the games. It'll be an all-day affair, I fear."

"Teenagers," Carrie said with a laugh. "I hope you survive."

"I hope *they* survive. My patience just isn't there anymore. What about you?"

Carrie stared out at the lake, her voice low. "Birthday party. James turns forty-five."

"You don't sound excited."

"It's a surprise party the boys and his mother insisted on. James hates surprise parties. He'll kill me."

"You could always secretly tell him," Jill suggested.

Carrie laughed. "Now there's an idea. But knowing James, he would simply refuse to get home in time for the alleged dinner at his mother's house."

"Then go with plan B—act as surprised as he is."

Carrie nodded, her smile causing the laugh lines around her eyes to show. "I like the way you think. That I might just try."

Jill shoved up the sleeve of her coat, glancing at her watch. She turned regretful eyes to Carrie.

"Time."

Carrie nodded. "I know."

"See you tomorrow?"

"For sure."

Jill nodded then turned, only to be stopped by a light touch on her arm. She paused, her eyes going first to the hand still resting on her sleeve, then to the eyes that waited for her. It was the first time they'd touched.

"Gonna steal my stocking cap or what?"

As their eyes held, Jill slowly nodded. "Yeah, I think I am."

Carrie let her hand slip off of Jill's arm, her blue eyes still holding Jill. She finally nodded too. "Then be my guest," she said quietly.

"I'll take care of it, don't worry," Jill said equally as quietly.

"I'm not worried. See you tomorrow."

As soon as Jill drove away, she slowly pulled the cap off her head, pausing to hold it to her face, breathing in what she assumed was Carrie's scent. She smiled and placed the cap securely in her lap as she headed back to work.

CHAPTER NINE

Jill drove carefully, wishing for a glass window between the front and backseat, anything to separate her from the squeals and shrieks of three gossiping teenage girls. But at least there was a smile on her daughter's face. Jill wasn't sure if it was because they were in Craig's new truck and not her old car or that Jill had treated them to burgers after the basketball games. Of course Craig would kill her if they got ketchup stains on the carpet, which would be a miracle if they did not, seeing how the girls were engrossed in stealing fries from one another.

"Oh, Mom, put that up louder. That's a cool song."

Jill cringed as she adjusted the volume, being subjected to yet another *cool* rap song. How the girls could tell one tune from the other, she had no clue. They all sounded alike to her. Then she smiled, wondering if her own mother had thought the same thing way back then, when Prince came on the radio and Jill and her friends all sang along.

Glancing at her watch, she tried to calculate when Craig would get home on the team's bus. For the use of his new truck, Jill had agreed to pick him up at school so he wouldn't have to drive her car. She suspected he was as embarrassed by the old Subaru as Angie was. A ride from school and steaks on the grill for dinner. That was the agreement. Steaks on the grill for the two of them. Angie was staying overnight at her friend's house.

Steaks and wine. Quiet. Romantic. Just the two of them.

Jill flicked her eyes to the rearview mirror, meeting her own for a brief moment before turning her attention back to the road. For some reason, the thought of having sex with Craig sent her into a panic. She had no idea what was wrong with her but she feared she would run from his touch.

Without warning, thoughts of Carrie crept into her mind. They'd been threatening all day but she shoved them aside, not understanding why she thought of the woman as much as she did. And not understanding why there was a terrible void on the weekends when she didn't see her. She saw her eyes again in the mirror, confused by her feelings, confused by her *attraction* to Carrie. Perhaps it was just her lack of a close female friendship that drew her to Carrie. Perhaps something was missing in her life and Carrie filled that need, whatever it was.

Again, she pushed thoughts of Carrie aside, concentrating on her driving instead.

"It's almost too cold to cook outside," Jill commented as she stood by dutifully while Craig got the grill going.

"One of these years, I'm going to build an outdoor fireplace," he said.

Jill laughed. "You say that every winter. I don't know why you won't just buy one."

He shrugged. "Why buy one when I can build one?"

Jill nodded, knowing as well as he did that he would never build one. "You want some more wine?" she asked.

"No. I'm not really crazy about this red wine. Not sweet enough for me."

"I love it."

"You must. You have a glass nearly every night."

Jill bristled. "Does that bother you?"

"No, babe. Hell, I know I'm hardly ever here at dinnertime. If you want to have a glass of wine, that's no problem."

"You're right. You're not here much. I've gotten fairly good at entertaining myself."

"I know. I'm sorry. It's just that time of year. Say, do we have any beer left in the fridge? I think I'll have that instead of this wine."

Jill silently watched him hurry into the house then turned, her eyes scanning the backyard, the trees still bare. She longed for spring, for warmer weather, for *green*. And she longed for companionship, for friendship, for conversation. She realized she and Craig no longer knew how to spend time together, no longer knew how to have a normal conversation. Yes, it was that time of year but every day was that time of year for him. Even in the summer, he could always find something, some *game*, to keep him away from home. As if anything would be better than Jill's company.

But that couldn't be true. It wasn't like they had a bad marriage. It wasn't like they argued and bickered. In fact, they seldom had a disagreement. No, she knew the truth for what it was. Her husband lived his life as he had in college. Everything revolved around sports. She knew it back then. But she'd assumed he would grow out of it.

She turned back to the house, seeing him through the windows as he talked on his cell phone, his hands moving animatedly, as if describing a shot. And no doubt he was. They'd won the tournament.

She was chilled from the night air but she had no desire to go back inside. So she filled her wineglass again then lifted the lid on the grill and robotically brushed the rack before putting on the two steaks. She turned the flame down low then moved to the porch swing, letting the motion relax her. She knew Craig had forgotten all about their steaks, had forgotten about her. He was in his element, talking to one of his buddies about the game. And later, when he remembered, he would rush out, apologizing for being on the phone so long. And she would tell him it was okay, she understood.

So she sat in the cold, quietly sipping her wine. She let visions of Carrie come to her without trying to stop them this time. They warmed her. She smiled slightly, remembering their parting conversation on Friday.

"Think of me Saturday night. I'll be suffering through a surprise birthday party."

"And think of me. I will have just suffered through two hours in the car with three teenagers!"

Carrie's eyes softened. "I always think about you."

Jill didn't know what to say. "I . . . I think about you too."

It was the truth. She just had no idea Carrie gave her a thought when they weren't together. She pushed off with her foot again, setting the swing in motion, wondering how the surprise party was going, wondering if Carrie was thinking of her.

And wondering if Carrie missed her today.

CHAPTER TEN

Jill watched the clock, the hands moving ever closer to one. The morning had been nearly insufferable and she urged the clock to hurry.

"You're being ridiculous," she murmured quietly. Yes, she knew she was. But she stood nonetheless, logging out of her computer before moving into the main office, waiting for Harriet to return so she could make her escape.

The sudden ringing of her cell phone startled her and she fished it out from inside her purse, frowning when she saw Craig's name displayed. He rarely called her.

"What's up?" she answered.

"Hey babe, glad I caught you."

She glanced quickly at the clock, then out through the windows to the street. "Is something wrong?"

"No, no, of course not. I thought maybe I'd take you to lunch today," he said.

She stopped short, panicked. "*What?* Lunch?"

"Yeah. I mean, I owe you 'cause of Saturday night."

She closed her eyes, letting her breath out slowly. The make-up lunch. She should have known.

"Craig, you have a class at one. You can't take me to lunch."

"I've got a student teacher with me this term. He's cool if I slip out."

She shook her head, then moved to the door when she saw Harriet drive in. "Craig, there's no need to take me to lunch. I don't want you to get into trouble."

"Babe, our football team went to State. My basketball team is in first place. I'm not going to get into trouble," he said with a laugh.

"Well, I don't *need* you to take me to lunch," she said quietly. "As a matter of fact, I'd just as soon you not."

"I knew you were mad. You said you weren't but I knew you were."

"I'm not mad. Really, I'm not. But my lunch is my time," she said evenly. "It's my time to relax and get away," she said, smiling as she met Harriet in the doorway. "So don't feel like you owe me."

"But I thought we could meet somewhere, maybe get a burger or something," he said.

She paused outside her car, glancing up into the overcast sky. "How about you take me and Angie out to dinner tonight? That'd be nice," she said.

"Oh, babe, I have practice after school. It'd be late."

She nodded. "Well, then how about the next night you have free? Maybe treat us to pizza or something."

"You sure?"

She unlocked her door and slipped inside, the phone tucked against her shoulder as she turned the key.

"I'm sure. Now go back to class."

She was five minutes late when she turned onto the park road and as her luck would have it, the rain that had been threatening all morning turned into a downpour in a matter of seconds.

"Unbelievable," she murmured as she slowed her speed, her wipers struggling to keep pace against the onslaught. She pulled into her normal parking place, wondering what she was going to do if she didn't see Carrie today. But she didn't have to wonder long. The other woman tapped on the passenger door and Jill unlocked it quickly.

They sat there, both smiling as Carrie brushed at the raindrops on her face.

"I think perhaps you bring the rain, my dear," Carrie said lightly.

Jill nodded. "It seems that's true."

"I love the rain."

Jill grinned. "I aim to please."

They were quiet, their eyes meeting, then moving away. Carrie finally cleared her throat.

"I . . . well, I missed you this weekend," she said.

Jill turned in her seat, looking into the pale blue eyes of her companion. She nodded slowly. "I missed you too."

Carrie cleared her throat again. "If you don't think it's too forward of me, may I suggest an alternative meeting place?"

Jill nodded, not caring in the least whether it sounded forward or not. Any alternative to sitting in her tiny Subaru in the rain was fine with her, as long as she got to see Carrie.

"I have a place on the lake, a small cottage," Carrie said. "Seems kinda odd for us to meet here, especially when it's foul weather, when we could be there," she finished with a shrug.

"You have a cottage? Here? No wonder you're familiar with the lake," Jill said.

Carrie flashed a grin. "Follow me. It's on the north side."

She was out before Jill could protest and Jill watched her through the foggy window as she got into a blue van. She backed up carefully and followed the van through the winding park road and back to the main highway. Instead of turning left, which would take her back to town, they turned right on a road that led them through the new subdivisions that had been creeping closer to the park. A few miles down the road, Carrie turned right again and Jill followed close behind. The tiny residential road was bumpy and Jill slowed, finally stopping as Carrie waited for an electric gate to open.

She followed Carrie through the gate, her Subaru bouncing nosily on the gravel road which curved dramatically through the trees. She saw the lake before she saw the cottage, her eyes widening as an inviting pier came into view. But she turned her attention back to the road, slowing again as the bumpy gravel road turned into a smooth paved driveway. She parked beside Carrie's van, pausing to grab her umbrella before getting out.

"This way," Carrie called, motioning for Jill to follow.

Through the white picket fence, a path led them to the back of the cottage and a sunporch. Jill paused to wipe her shoes on the mat before following Carrie inside.

"Just leave your umbrella there by the door," Carrie said. "I'll turn the heat on."

Jill nodded, shivering as the damp cold penetrated. She turned in a circle in the sunroom, a smile forming as she looked at the lake. The sunroom had a perfect view of the lake and pier.

"You like?"

She turned at the sound of Carrie's voice, nodding. "Beautiful."

"Not so much now. Everything is gray, dull. Even the water. But springtime is beautifully green, it almost hurts your eyes," she said.

Jill spread her arms. "If you have this, why bother with the park?"

Carrie shrugged. "Can't sketch the same old stuff every day, now can I?"

"Yeah, but you wouldn't have to put up with—" Jill stopped, smiling. "Maybe I really don't like people after all."

Carrie laughed. "I enjoy the privacy of this place too. Especially in the summer, when kids run amuck at the park." She pointed to the door she'd just come through. "Want a tour?"

"Of course."

"Won't take long though. I didn't build this for a family home. It's just a place I can escape to."

Jill followed her into the cottage, the bright walls a contrast to the dark, dreary day outside. A long bar separated the kitchen from the den and Carrie scooted a barstool closer to the bar as they passed.

"A nice-sized kitchen but I don't really use it much," Carrie said. She pointed to the sitting area, which was sparsely furnished. "Or this. I mostly use the sunporch."

"I love the kitchen. It looks inviting." Jill turned to face her. "How long have you had it?"

"I built it four years ago." She laughed. "As you can see, I don't come here all that much."

"I'd be here every day. Do you guys spend weekends here?"

Carrie shook her head. "James and the boys have no idea it exists."

Jill stared. "Why not?"

Carrie smiled. "Because I haven't told them."

"How in world can your husband not know?"

"We keep our finances separate." She laughed. "Well, not really. I mean, he's made a small fortune with his business—okay, a large fortune—so my real estate profits were my play money, as he called it. And as an agent, I didn't sell all that much, so it really was play money. But I never told him how much I made on the property I bought on a whim all those years ago."

"What property?"

"Here at the lake." She pointed to a closed door. "Bedroom's through there. And I've never used it." She opened another door. "Large bathroom. It's got a connecting door to the bedroom."

"Nice. I like the red."

"It'll wake you up, that's for sure." She sat on one corner of the tiny loveseat, motioning for Jill to join her. "Years ago, the park was just an afterthought, really. There were a handful of homes on the south side, closer to town, and that was it. The county owned most of the rest but the lake was built as a water reservoir and for fishing. They weren't really pushing development then.

"But anyway, I was pregnant with Josh, so nearly eighteen years ago I was fishing out in a canoe on the north side of the lake. There was this old man fishing on a pier, little bitty pier and I waved to him. He took one look at me and stood up. 'What in tarnation do you think you're doing?'" Carrie laughed as she mimicked him. "Honest to God, that's what he said. So I'm looking around, wondering if there's some easement or something in the lake and I was trespassing. So I told him I was fishing. He pointed to his pier and said get over here right now. I know I probably should've been afraid, I mean, he was six-foot tall, easy. But I looked at him and said 'yes, sir,' and paddled over. I sat there in my canoe and he pointed at me. 'Good God, girl, you're about to give birth. What were you thinking? That I'd swim on out to help you when you went into labor? Now get out of that there boat!'" Carrie smiled fondly. "Oh, he was a character. He drove me around to the park in his old, beat-up truck and got my car, then we drove back to collect my canoe."

"How in the world did you lift a canoe when you were nine months pregnant?"

"I was *praying* I'd go into labor," she said with a laugh. "But he was such a sweet man. He was eighty-six and a widower. And he owned a couple hundred acres he didn't know what to do with. We became friends. I was quite taken with him. I spent every day after that with him, until I gave birth. His name was

Joshua."

"You named your son after him."

"Yes. James had his heart set on Jeremy. I convinced him to change it. But anyway, Joshua sold me all his property, except for about ten acres that his house sat on. I never told James. And I never did anything with it. But I'd go visit him often, always taking Josh with me. Josh wasn't even two when he died. He didn't have any kids of his own and he left me the rest of his property."

"Wow."

Carrie shrugged. "Kinda strange I never told James, I suppose. I just hung on to it, sneaking out whenever I could. It was my escape. But then the developers came and I didn't know what I was going to do with two hundred acres. So I sold for an outrageous amount of money about five years ago."

"And James never knew?"

"No. I retired on the pretense I wanted to spend more time with the boys and I wanted to take some art classes. I tore down Joshua's old shack and pier, and built this little cottage. It won't be much for resale, not with just the one bedroom. But it's just a place I can come to, if I need it."

"Like for lunch on rainy days?"

"Like for lunch on any day. Unless you have a fondness for the park and all its people," Carrie teased.

"I'd rather come here," Jill said seriously. "I mean, if you want," she added.

Carrie nodded. "The sunroom is wonderful when the weather's bad. The pier is awesome when the weather is nice."

"Do the ducks make it around this far?"

"There are some that hang around but I'm not here enough to feed them on a regular basis, so they're not always here. But I've never seen Grandma Duck out this far." Carrie reached over and squeezed her arm. "If you're going to miss feeding the ducks, we'll have to make a date to meet at the park at least once a week."

"Well, like you, I've become fond of Grandma Duck." Her eyes lingered where Carrie's hand still touched and she wished she wasn't wearing long sleeves. She watched as Carrie's fingers slipped away, then looked up, meeting Carrie's eyes for a brief moment.

"It's probably getting late," Carrie said.

Jill nodded then pushed up her sleeve, revealing the slim watch she wore. She nodded again.

"Yes. Time."

"Well, maybe the weather will be nicer tomorrow. I'll show you the pier and garden." She stood. "And maybe I'll surprise you with lunch."

CHAPTER ELEVEN

"I know you love the rain but four days in a row is a bit much," Jill complained as they sat in the sunroom and munched on the burgers and fries she'd picked up on her way over.

"Green. Think green."

"I'm beyond that. I'm trying to remember what sunshine looks like." Jill grinned. "Do you think we should start building a boat?"

"No. We'll use my canoe to escape," Carrie said seriously, then wiggled her eyebrows teasingly.

"But this is really nice, isn't it. I can't believe how warm the sunroom stays. I could almost convince myself this is a spring rain and not winter."

"Spring will be here soon enough. And I think this year I'll tend to the garden. It was Joshua's pride and joy. When I had his old shack torn down, I made sure to leave the garden undisturbed.

When they landscaped the flower beds around here, I had them weed and mulch his garden. It looked great that first year." Carrie smiled. "I just don't have Joshua's green thumb."

"Well, maybe this spring, we could steal a Saturday and . . . and maybe plant some flowers," Jill suggested. "I mean, if you could sneak away from your family for a day."

Carrie's pale eyes looked into her own for a long moment before answering.

"And can you sneak away from your family?"

Jill nodded. "I think I'm allowed a day out now and then." She paused, brows drawn together. "You know, I've not mentioned you to Craig. I mean, we've become friends and I've not even mentioned your name to him."

Carrie nodded. "Is that odd?"

"Yes. Don't you think?"

Carrie's lips just hinted at a smile. "I don't think it's odd. I've not told James about you either."

Jill leaned forward. "Why is that, do you think?"

"I don't think it really concerns him. Our friendship is . . . well, it's just between us. I didn't feel the need to share you with him."

Jill nodded. "Yes. I think that's how I feel. I don't want to have to share anything we do or say. It's just us."

It was quiet in the sunroom as Jill's words hung in the air. *It's just us.* She had an odd feeling as those words echoed around in her brain. *Just us.* She had been on the verge of mentioning Carrie to Craig on a few occasions but something told her not to. So she kept her new friendship to herself, not for a moment thinking that Carrie had done the same.

She looked up, not surprised to find Carrie's eyes on her. She was surprised, however, by the warm sensation that traveled across her body as she let herself be pulled into those blue depths.

"It would be nice to be able to spend more than an hour

together," Carrie said quietly. "Perhaps in a few weeks, if the weather warms, we could—"

"Clean flowerbeds?" Jill suggested.

"I promise I'll feed you."

Jill's smile was warm as she reached out and lightly touched Carrie's hand. "Then it's a date."

Those words hung between them as Jill slowly removed her fingers from Carrie's hand.

CHAPTER TWELVE

It was unusually quiet as Jill closed the back door and moved silently across the deck. She supposed the cold rain of earlier had chased everyone inside for the evening. She took a deep breath, smelling wood smoke from neighboring chimneys. A romantic concept, but she and Craig had yet to have one this winter. Of course, a cheery fire burning warmly inside usually meant some-one was there to enjoy it. And on this evening, like so many others, she was alone. Craig and Angie were at the basketball game. To their credit, they had invited her. It was an after-thought on Craig's part, she knew, but nonetheless, he'd offered and she declined.

She moved to the porch swing, sinking down heavily as she put it in motion. Her fingers were cold on the wineglass and she pulled her robe tighter around her.

The cold . . . the quiet. A year ago, loneliness would have

settled upon her by now. A feeling of . . . well, not quite depression, just an aloneness, a feeling she lived with, grew to recognize, grew to accept.

But tonight, as she sat in the swing and quietly rocked back and forth, she couldn't quite conjure up that feeling. She felt at peace. She felt . . . connected.

She tilted her head back, her eyes searching through the bare trees to the sky, finding only a handful of stars that escaped from behind the clouds. It was enough. She smiled, letting her eyes slip closed as she thought of Carrie, a woman she'd known barely six weeks.

Again, a sense of peace settled over her. She was past trying to figure out why she felt so drawn to Carrie. It didn't matter. She simply was.

She suspected the feeling was mutual.

And that scared her a little.

How long she sat out in the cold, she had no idea. Long enough for the wine bottle to be nearly empty, long enough for the neighbor's lights to go out. She knew she should go inside but she couldn't seem to find the energy to move. But only minutes later, she saw headlights flash across the trees, then the sound of the garage door opening.

She sighed, knowing her peace was over. She swallowed the last of the wine in her glass then bent over to pick up the bottle. She heard Craig calling for her and it was only then she realized she hadn't left any lights on inside. Before she could get up, Craig opened the back door, seeing her in the shadows.

"Jill? What are you doing?"

"Just . . . just sitting."

"But it's freezing out here."

She pulled her robe tighter around her. "I hadn't noticed."

He surprised her by coming out onto the deck and joining

her on the porch swing. Putting an arm around her shoulders, he drew her closer to him.

"Good game?" she asked, trying not to stiffen in his arms.

"Oh, yeah. We killed them, babe. You should come sometime. I really think this is the year we go to State. We're that damn good."

"I'll make a game, I promise."

"Yeah, you always say that."

"I just felt like being alone tonight."

He put the swing in motion then squeezed her shoulder again.

"You've felt like being alone a lot lately," he said quietly.

"You think so? Just because I didn't want to go to your game?"

"No. It's just, you know, you come out here a lot. Sit out here by yourself. What's going on, Jill?"

"Nothing. Nothing's going on."

"You sure? I mean is there something I need to worry about?"

She smiled. "What are you asking, Craig?"

"You just haven't seemed very happy lately. Makes me think you're not happy with me."

She sighed. "I don't know what's wrong, Craig." She shrugged. "I just feel like being alone is all." She laughed nervously. "I'll be forty in a few months. Maybe it's that."

"But it's not . . . it's not another man?"

She pulled away slightly, staring at him. "Another man? No, it's not another man." She poked him with her elbow. "In *this* town? Are you kidding me?"

His laugh was filled with relief she noted as he pulled her closer and kissed her quickly on the lips.

"Okay then. Good. And we have a lunch date tomorrow," he said.

She frowned. "A date?"

"Yeah. No school. Teacher's workday. I promised Angie I'd

take the two of you for pizza. I still owe you, you know."

"But—"

"No buts. I'll swing by here and pick up Angie and then we'll pick you up." He grinned. "I can't remember the last time we went to lunch together. It'll be fun."

Fun? She took a deep breath, trying to shake off the panic that was threatening. Tomorrow was Friday. Her last chance to see Carrie before the weekend.

CHAPTER THIRTEEN

Jill watched the ticking of the clock. On more than one occasion, she'd picked up the phone intending to call Craig, intending to make up some excuse to cancel their lunch date. And each time, she hung up before it could ring. She could think of no plausible reason to cancel.

So she spent the rest of the morning trying to think of a way to contact Carrie. She had almost talked herself into driving out to the cottage and leaving a note but decided that was a bit much. Of course, it would all be so much simpler if she and Carrie had at least exchanged phone numbers. As it was, Carrie would simply be left to wonder if Jill decided to skip out on their daily lunch or . . . or what? Got a better offer? She glanced out the window at the sunshine that had finally made an appearance after four days of rain. A better offer? It wouldn't be possible.

She looked again to the clock, knowing Harriet would be

leaving soon. Then she would have an hour to herself, a whole hour to wish she had no lunch date with her husband.

"Oh, Jill, what is wrong with you?" she whispered. She cupped her face in her hands and let out a deep breath. Indeed, what was wrong with her? How could she possibly be dreading seeing her husband and daughter?

Oh, it wasn't that she was dreading the lunch date. She knew the truth for what it was. She was dreading *not* being able to see Carrie. It wasn't startling to realize she would rather spend her lunch hour with Carrie, not her husband. She would rather spend it talking and visiting and getting to know her new friend, not sitting in a crowded pizza joint with high school kids all clamoring for attention, her daughter included.

But she would go. She would pretend to have a good time. And at two, when Craig dropped her off at the office, she would kiss him good-bye and tell him how much she enjoyed it. Then the rest of the afternoon would crawl by, much like the morning had, and this empty feeling in her stomach would grow and grow as the weekend approached.

"I don't know why we couldn't have come at noon," Angie complained. "All the cool kids are already gone."

"Because my lunch time is one to two," Jill said as she reached for a slice of pizza.

"I should have asked you to switch, I guess," Craig said. As Jill stared at him, eyebrows raised, he shrugged. "It's her lunch too."

"Oh, look, Dad, isn't that Lance?" Angie asked quietly.

Jill followed their gaze. "Lance who?"

Angie rolled her eyes dramatically. "He's only like the coolest, Mom. Hello? Quarterback?"

"Oh, of course. *That* Lance. Isn't he a senior?"

"So? It's not like I'm a child, you know."

"Of course not. What was I thinking?"

Craig laughed. "He's got a girlfriend, Angie. Patti Helms."

"Only 'cause she's a cheerleader," Angie said, her face screwing up as if she'd just sucked on a lemon.

Jill bit her lip to keep from laughing as the object of Angie's lust walked past.

"Hey, Coach."

"Lance, how's it going?"

An inaudible grunt was the response as he headed to the buffet table. Angie's eyes never left him.

"Cute and an extensive vocabulary too," Jill teased. However, neither Craig nor Angie heard. Both of their cell phones rang at once.

Jill sat quietly—patiently—as Angie's voice lowered to a whisper as she relayed her chance encounter with the quarterback to one of her friends. Craig's voice was as loud and animated as always when he talked sports. She turned away, her glance going to the windows, finding the sunshine, wishing she was out in it. It was warm enough. They might have even braved the pier for the first time.

She sighed, her shoulders sagging as she tuned out the voices of the others around her. Amazing how lonely she could feel sitting in the presence of her husband and daughter. She closed her eyes for a moment then attempted to conceal her frustration with a smile. Neither of them noticed as they continued with their conversations.

Taking her nearly empty glass of tea, she walked slowly to the counter, refilling her glass and adding a slice of lemon before turning around again. Amazing, but Craig didn't even seem to notice that she wasn't there. Had it always been this way and she'd just never noticed before?

She nodded. Yes, it had. And yes, she noticed. She'd just never cared before. She was content to get lost in her own thoughts, to people-watch . . . whatever. So then why did it matter now? Why did she want his attention now?

Again, she didn't run from the truth. And the truth was, she was afraid. Afraid of her interest in Carrie. Afraid of the attention Carrie showed her. And perhaps if she and Craig talked more, spent more time together, then Carrie wouldn't constantly be on her mind. And perhaps she wouldn't wish she was with Carrie instead of her husband.

Like now.

She stood there and watched them from a distance, wondering who Craig was talking to, who held his attention. Angie's call had ended and she'd gone to the buffet for a couple more slices of pizza. She watched as Craig snapped his fingers at her and pointed to his own plate, indicating he wanted more too. Jill's eyes shifted to her abandoned plate, seeing the half-eaten piece she'd started on, and the second, still untouched.

She made herself move, walking back to their table, touching Craig lightly on the shoulder as she passed. He looked at her and smiled, then went back to his conversation.

"Aren't you going to eat?" Angie asked as she plopped another piece of pizza on her father's plate.

Jill stared at her plate again then shook her head. "Not really hungry anymore."

"Who's he talking to anyway?"

"I have no idea," Jill said quietly. She shoved the sleeve up on her arm, noting the time. She tapped her fingers quietly on the table for a few seconds then finally nudged Craig.

"Yeah, hang on a sec, Brad," he said, covering the phone with his palm. "What is it, babe?"

"As much as I've enjoyed our lunch date together, I need to get back."

"Is it time already?"

She stared at him for a moment then shoved her chair back as she stood. When she glanced at her daughter, she was surprised to see a hint of understanding in her eyes. She nodded slightly then walked out the door and into the sunshine. She bent her head back, staring into the blueness above, the clouds long ago chased from the sky.

"Sorry about that, babe," Craig said as he held the truck door open for her. "That was Brad from the radio station. They want to interview me before our game on Tuesday."

"How nice," she murmured.

When he closed his own door, he turned to Angie in the back and gave her a smile. "It was good to all go out together, wasn't it?" He turned to Jill. "Right?"

She smiled. "Sure, Craig. It was nice to spend time with you."

Jill sat quietly at her desk, her door closed. She moved the mouse absently, the screen saver fading away as she watched. She tilted her head, staring at the monitor as the jumble of numbers ran together. Closing her eyes, she shoved away from the desk, turning her chair toward the window.

She couldn't concentrate on work.

Wonder what she did for lunch? Wonder if she went out to the pier?

"Wonder if she missed me being there?" Jill murmured.

A quick tap on her door brought her around. "What is it?"

Harriet stuck her head inside. "There's a call for you."

Harriet closed the door behind her and Jill stared at the phone, seeing the one blinking line and knowing instinctively that it was Carrie. The pounding of her pulse told her that. So, taking a deep breath, she answered in her most professional tone.

"Jill Richardson. How may I help you?"

A pause, then, "Are you okay?"

Jill squeezed the phone tightly. "No. I mean, yeah, I'm okay, but . . . no."

Carrie laughed quietly. "Surprisingly, I understand completely."

Jill smiled. "Craig took me and Angie out for lunch. Pizza. I didn't know about it until last night. And I didn't have any way of contacting you."

"It's okay. You don't have to explain. I was just worried. I had visions of you having a car accident or something."

"I'm sorry."

"There's nothing to be sorry for."

"Yes there is. I'm sorry I missed our lunch," Jill said quietly.

There was silence and Jill could picture Carrie's face, could almost see her pale blue eyes.

"I understand husbands come first."

Jill closed her eyes as she pressed the phone tightly against her ear. "I would have rather . . . well, I wish I had been at the cottage with you."

"I missed you too, Jill."

Jill could hear the smile in Carrie's voice and she smiled too. "I've grown to hate weekends."

The laughter in her ear brought a quick grin to her face, chasing away the quiet desperation she'd felt most of the day.

"Well, perhaps soon we'll be able to steal a Saturday."

Jill leaned back in her chair, still clutching the phone tightly. "What did you do today?" she asked quietly.

"Well, after I realized you weren't going to come, I drove to the park to feed the ducks. I think Grandma Duck has missed us this week. But it was such a nice day, there were lots of people about." She laughed again. "You would have hated it."

"Trust me, I would have loved it."

CHAPTER FOURTEEN

Jill rolled over, her eyes half opened as she took a quick peek at the clock. She leaned up on her elbow, frowning.

"Oh, crap," she murmured. It was seven forty-five. She tossed the covers off then stopped. "It's Saturday. It's freakin' Saturday."

She lay back down with a groan, eyes wide open as she stared at the ceiling. Saturday. Not a work day.

"Saturday," she whispered. "I hate Saturdays."

With a sigh, she closed her eyes again, hoping sleep would claim her, hoping it would take her away for a few more hours. But it didn't. She'd never been a late sleeper. And try as she may, she apparently wasn't going to start now.

"Crap," she murmured again as she swung her legs off the bed. She sat there for awhile, staring at the wall, staring at nothing. She finally stood and slipped her feet into the moccasins she slipped off last night. As she walked past the bed, she grabbed her robe off the banister and slipped it on.

She was halfway down the stairs when she heard rustling in the kitchen. She stopped, silently hoping he wasn't making a mess of things. But she did smell coffee. That was a start.

She pushed on the swinging door, nearly knocking Craig off his feet as he walked by with a handful of eggs.

"Good God, you're cooking?"

"Don't act so surprised."

"I've just never seen you do it before," she said as she sidestepped him to get to the coffee.

"Now that's not true. When Angie was a baby, I remember a couple of times I got up early to make breakfast."

Jill smiled. "She's nearly fifteen."

Craig laughed. "Don't let her hear you say that. She's *fourteen* and not a day older."

Jill leaned against the counter and sipped from her coffee, watching as he cracked eggs and dropped them into the pan.

"If I want these scrambled, I just kinda stir them up, right?"

"At this point, yes. Most people scramble them prior to the pan."

Craig waved a spatula at her. "Just a waste of a bowl."

"May I ask why you're making breakfast?"

He grinned. "Don't you know?"

She frowned. *Oh God, it wasn't their anniversary, was it?* No. June. *Birthday?* No. July.

"Oh, come on," he said. "It's the make-up breakfast."

She shook her head. "For what?"

He shrugged. "For the make-up lunch."

"How so?"

"You know, yesterday at lunch, I got a phone call."

"And?"

"And, well, we didn't really have the family lunch I'd planned."

She tilted her head as she looked at him. "You came to this

conclusion all on your own?"

"Well, no. Not exactly."

Jill smiled. "Angie thought I was mad?"

"Yeah." He stirred the eggs then quickly looked back at her. "Are you?"

"Not mad, no." She forced a smile. "I never could compete with your cell phone."

He moved to the toaster and put two slices of bread in, then opened the fridge and pulled out the jug of orange juice. He looked at her with eyebrows raised and she nodded.

"I thought, you know, maybe today we could have a day out."

"What kind of a day out?" she asked suspiciously, watching as he poured their juice.

"Well, I thought maybe we could drive over to Richland."

"Richland? Why on earth?"

"Well, they're hosting a basketball tournament."

"I see. And?"

"I kinda wanted to see it. You know, we play Richland next week."

She opened the cabinet and took out two plates, silently handing them to him, before opening the drawer to the utensils.

"Well, you know what, I don't really want to go to Richland to watch a basketball game," she said. "Why don't you ask one of your buddies to go? You know, guys day out," Jill suggested.

He grabbed the toast and tossed them on the plates, then handed one to her.

"Are you sure?"

She nodded. "I'm sure."

"But what will you do?"

She reached for her coffee, taking a sip before answering. "Boring as it sounds, I need to go to the grocery store. Not to mention laundry."

"Oh, babe, that's work. I'm offering you a free day. No work."

She raised her eyebrows. "So who's going to do it if I don't?"

The trip to the grocery store was made with practiced ease and she methodically checked items off her list as she moved down each aisle. But it wasn't groceries on her mind. She had a free day. A free Saturday.

And still, she and Carrie had yet to exchange phone numbers. But if they had, Jill would call her, see if maybe they could get together for a few hours today. Maybe even go to the cottage and sit down at the pier. It was another sunny day. And although it was far too early for spring fever, she had a desire to be outside, to sit in the sun. A desire to see Carrie.

Frowning, wondering why this woman was *always* on her mind, she stopped and looked at her list, trying to muster up some enthusiasm to finish her task.

Afterward, she would go home, have a quiet lunch then perhaps enjoy the sunshine on her own patio. And maybe her mind wouldn't be filled with thoughts of Carrie.

Later, as she pulled into her driveway, her backseat covered with grocery bags, she was surprised to see her mother-in-law coming out of the side door.

"Why Jill, I didn't expect you to be here."

Jill bit her lip to keep the obvious retort from slipping out. It was one thing for Craig's parents to have a key to their home for emergencies. It was quite another that Arlene felt the need to use it any time she liked.

"Grocery store," she said as she opened the back door and pulled out two bags.

"Grocery store? I would have thought you'd gone to Richland with Craig."

"Why?"

Arlene pursed her lips and Jill prepared herself for the lecture she was about to get.

"You and Craig hardly spend any time together as it is. I would think you'd want to be with your husband."

"My *husband* was going to a basketball tournament, Arlene. As you know, I'm not really crazy about basketball."

"But Craig loves basketball."

"Yes, but I don't. I didn't want to waste my Saturday doing something I hate."

"I hardly think riding with your husband to a game would be considered wasting your time."

Jill opened her mouth then closed it again. She wouldn't waste her time now by arguing with Arlene. So she walked past her, pushing open the side door with her shoulder.

"Did you need something, Arlene?"

"Oh, I baked cakes yesterday. I brought one over. You know how much Craig likes my German chocolate cake."

"Yes. So does Angie. I'm sure they'll love it."

"I wish you would learn to bake, Jill. Craig has always loved desserts. I'm sure he would appreciate a fresh-baked cake every now and then."

Jill smiled. "Yes, and he appreciates when you bring them over." She walked back outside, getting the rest of her bags from the backseat.

"Well, baking does take some talent. Unless you open up a box and use a cake mix. Then I say, what's the point?"

"Yes, well, thanks, Arlene. I'll be sure to try a piece myself."

Arlene stood in the kitchen, watching as Jill put the groceries away. Jill finally stopped. "Was there something else, Arlene?"

"No. I guess I should get going. It's nearly lunchtime." She paused on her way out. "Do you want to join us? Carl is grilling burgers."

Jill shook her head. "No, but thanks."

"No trouble to do one for you."

"Actually, I've got some errands to run. I'll pick up something in town," she lied.

"Okay then. And don't forget, we're having steaks for dinner. If this weather holds, it'll be nice to cook out."

Jill frowned, her eyebrows pulling together. "Craig didn't mention we were having dinner with you tonight."

"He didn't? Yes, at seven. But don't worry about bringing anything. It'll be simple. I'll do baked potatoes."

Jill nodded. "Well, I'm glad you told me. I would have already started dinner by the time he got home."

Arlene moved to leave then stopped again. "Where's Angie?"

"She's at Shelly's house. Her mother was taking them to the movies today, then she's staying over."

"How fun. It must be nice for you, hmmm?"

"What do you mean?"

"Oh, that Angie doesn't bring her friends over here. That way, you don't have to play mom."

Jill was about to protest but she didn't. It was the truth. Angie rarely brought her friends over to the house. So she nodded. "I think she's afraid I'd have to haul them around in my old car."

"It's no wonder she thinks you don't like her. You spend even less time with her than you do your husband." She looked back over her shoulder. "See you tonight."

Alone again, Jill finished unpacking her groceries, trying not to let Arlene get to her. She wasn't certain if she said things on purpose or if she was completely oblivious as to how hurtful her words were.

Slamming the cabinet door harder than necessary, she stood there, hands tightly gripping the counter. Without another thought, she grabbed her purse, going back outside into the sunshine. Before she knew it, she was speeding down the street, driving automatically, watching the familiar sights of their small city zip by as she headed out of town.

And toward the lake.

She didn't know how she knew it but something was guiding her, as if she was a puppet in a play. She had no reason to think that Carrie would be at the cottage on a Saturday. Yet, that's where she was headed, not for a moment questioning her reasoning.

That was why, a short time later, she was not surprised to find the gate open as she bounced along the tiny road. She felt an instant wave of relief when she saw Carrie's blue van parked in the driveway.

As she stood outside, she debated whether to use the front door or to go around the back to the sunroom like they normally did.

"Well, what a pleasant surprise."

Jill turned at the sound of Carrie's voice, her smile matching that of the other woman.

"You know, if you leave your gate open like that, you never know who will drop by."

Carrie walked closer, her eyes turning serious. "Would you believe me if I told you I had this . . . this feeling that you'd come today?"

Jill let herself be pulled into Carrie's eyes. She nodded. "Yes, I would believe you." She laughed lightly, pulling her eyes away from Carrie's, breaking the spell the woman seemed to have on her. "We've *really* got to exchange phone numbers."

"Yes, we do." She pulled off her gardening gloves and wiped her hands on her jeans. "Because this day is too beautiful not to share." She motioned for Jill to follow as she walked through the picket fence and around to the back. "Let me wash up, then we can go sit down at the pier."

"You're sure I'm not intruding?"

"Oh, absolutely not. It was just so pretty out, I thought it'd be a good day to start on the flowerbeds." She went to the sink in the kitchen to wash and Jill pulled out a bar stool, watching. "How did you sneak away?"

"Didn't have to sneak. There wasn't anyone at home."

"Oh yeah?"

Jill sighed. "Craig went to a basketball tournament in Richland." She waved her hand dismissively. "He wanted me to go with him so we could spend some time together."

"And?"

"I declined. For one thing, I hate basketball. And two, as long as his cell phone is with him, there's not a moment of down time."

"You hate basketball and he's a coach? How did that happen?"

"Football, basketball and baseball. He coaches all three. Football is the only one I have any interest in. But he lives for them all."

"How in the world can he possibly coach all three?"

"Assistant coach in football, head coach in basketball. He's the hitting coach for the baseball team. And yes, it takes up most of his time. Sports, period, take up most of his time." She shook her head. "I don't mean to complain. He was like this when I married him. I just thought he'd have outgrown it by now."

Carrie leaned on the bar with her elbows, watching Jill. When their eyes met, Jill tilted her head.

"What?"

"I just think it's kind of odd that we both have husbands so busy with their own lives that we've become almost an after-thought." She shrugged. "At least, that's how I feel sometimes."

Jill nodded. "Exactly. Yesterday, when he took us out for lunch, his cell rang barely ten minutes into it. I think he actually forgot I was even there. I had to ask him to end the call just so he could take me back to work."

"I know what you mean. I think James would shrivel up and die if he lost his cell phone. But I try not to complain. It wasn't all that many years ago where mine was the one constantly ringing." She moved to the fridge and held it open, peering inside. "Have you had lunch?"

"No. You?"

"No. But I don't have much to offer." She smiled over the top of the door. "Cheese and crackers that we had last week."

"That's fine."

"And I've got a bottle of wine. How about we spend the afternoon down at the pier?"

"Wonderful. It'll be nice to visit without having to watch the time." Jill stood, then paused. "Or do you have to get back?"

Carrie shook her head. "I'm all yours."

"I can't believe she said that to you. My mother-in-law would never interfere like that," Carrie said. "Even though I'm sure she's wanted to on occasion."

"Most of my shortcomings usually involve Angie but today she was focusing on Craig too. I really think the woman hates me."

"I'm telling you, it's because he's an only child. In her mind, no woman will ever be good enough for her baby."

"I know. I keep telling myself that," Jill said, holding out her glass for Carrie to refill. "Thanks. But I sometimes wonder if there's not some truth to what she says. We hardly spend any time together as it is. And I mean, even though I hate basketball, shouldn't I be more supportive and go to his games? I know other wives do."

"Did you in the beginning?"

Jill nodded. "Yeah. I used to make all the home games, at least. But it just became a chore. Something I hated to do. I was resenting the fact that on *my* time, I felt obligated to follow him around like some groupie." She laughed nervously. "God, that sounds so awful."

"It doesn't matter how it sounds. You should be able to voice your feelings, Jill."

"Yeah, but it sounds so selfish. I mean, what's wrong with me? Why don't I want to spend time with him?"

"Is that what you think it is?"

"I don't know anymore."

Carrie looked out over the lake then stretched her legs out as she got more comfortable on the bench. Jill turned sideways, watching her.

"I often wonder how my own marriage survived," Carrie said. "But in the beginning, I was the one never at home. Every weekend, I was out showing houses, meeting buyers and sellers alike, never home for James, never home for the boys. It's just a miracle my kids have turned out to be such sweethearts." She turned slowly, meeting Jill's eyes. "Then, of course, the stores took off and James was gone all the time." She turned back to the lake. "And our kids still love us."

"What school do they go to? It's not Kline, is it?"

Carrie shook her head. "Private school. Brookhaven." She held her hands out as if to catch the sunshine. "Such a gorgeous day. I'm so glad you're here to share it with me." She smiled. "And it's good to see you like this, in everyday clothes. You look comfortable. You look nice."

Jill blushed then rubbed her hands on her jeans. "I hate business suits but Mr. Tutt insisted on them. Now that his son runs the business, he's not as particular but I've already got a closet full of them."

"That's the first thing I did when I got out of the real estate business. I tossed all my suits. I swore I'd never put on another pair of high-heeled shoes." She picked up the wine bottle and held it up. "We've about killed it." She laughed. "God, I love lazy days like this."

"Yes. It's so nice out here." Jill reached over and touched her hand. "Where are your boys today? How is it that you're alone?"

Carrie stared at their hands for a long moment then raised her eyes. Jill went to pull her hand away, embarrassed, but Carrie stopped her.

"You only wear a wedding band," Carrie said quietly.

Jill raised her eyebrows.

"No diamond, just the band," Carrie explained, touching her ring finger. She held up her own left hand. "Me too."

Jill nodded. "Craig and I couldn't afford much when we got engaged. I didn't see the point in spending an obscene amount of money on a diamond when we didn't even have a house to live in."

"You got married in college?"

"No. A month later. We both graduated in May. Got married in June. Started teaching—both at Kline—in August." She shook her head with a smile. "A whirlwind summer."

"Why here?"

Jill shrugged. "Craig's from here."

Carrie gave her a sympathetic smile. "I can't believe your in-laws live three doors down."

Jill laughed. "Most days, neither can I."

Jill turned her attention to the lake and stretched out, much like Carrie was doing. The garden bench was small and she was aware that their hands still brushed, aware each time Carrie's fingers moved across her skin. She finally turned, not surprised to find Carrie's eyes on her. Their eyes held for a long moment. Again, that feeling of familiarity—of connecting—settled around her. She liked it. It felt peaceful.

"I'm really glad you came today," Carrie said quietly.

"Me too."

"I wish we could do this more often."

Jill nodded and smiled. "Perhaps we should exchange phone numbers," she suggested.

"And I'll give you the code to the gate. Because even if we can't be together, there's no reason you can't come out here and enjoy the peace and quiet."

"Oh, I wouldn't come out if you weren't here."

"Why not? I'm offering. Besides, you are the only other soul who even knows this place exists."

Jill paused. "Do you feel guilty you've not shared this with your family?"

Carrie shook her head. "No, not at all. For one thing, James could never slow down enough to enjoy it out here. He's all go, go, go, all the time. Now the boys would probably enjoy the lake in the summer, would enjoy going swimming, but they both have their own things going on now. Josh will graduate in May and go off to college. He doesn't have a clue as to what he wants to do but he wants to leave home, go someplace new. And I'm all for that. He's far too young to be stuck in one place. But Aaron, now he's his father's son. He so smart, he could do anything he wanted—engineering, computer science, anything. But damn if he doesn't want to stay here and run one of James's stores."

"Well, I'm sure James is happy at least one of them wants to follow in his footsteps," Jill said.

"Oh, of course he is. I think he was secretly afraid he was working his ass off all these years for nothing," she said with a laugh. "But in the summers, Aaron goes with him every day. And this coming summer, James has promised him an assistant manager's job. I have this horrible fear he'll graduate high school and move into a manager's position and never go to college. And Aaron would be perfectly happy. So would James, for that matter."

"Well, at least your kids have interests. Angie's world revolves around boys and makeup. I know she's only a freshman but she shows no interest in anything. I asked her once what she wanted to do and she said she'd probably end up being a secretary, like me," Jill said with a smirk.

Carrie laughed and squeezed Jill's hand.

"I know. If she knew my salary was more than her father's, she'd die. I don't know how it happened but she's very old-fashioned." Jill leaned closer, liking the feel of Carrie's fingers on her hand. "She has this vision of fathers working to support the family and mothers being home to cater to the kids. And I know she gets that from her grandmother."

"She spends a lot of time with her?"

"Yes. Especially when she was younger. After school, she'd go over there until I got home from work. Even now that she's older, she still goes over after school most days. I cringe when I think of all the crap they must be filling her head with."

"Does Craig know all the things his mother says to you?"

"No. In the beginning when she'd say something to piss me off, I'd tell him, but usually he would just laugh it off, or worse, take her side. The only time he didn't take her side was when I quit teaching. He knew how miserable I was."

"So you tolerate her and pretend everything's fine?"

"Yes. And she informed me we're having dinner with them tonight. Craig apparently forgot to tell me."

"Ouch."

"Yeah. What a way to end a perfect day."

"Was it a perfect day?" Carrie asked quietly.

Jill smiled. "Well, let's see? It didn't start out all that great, no. But sitting here at the lake in the sunshine, visiting with you . . . yeah, it was perfect."

"I'm glad you think so."

But after sitting through dinner, silently listening as Craig gave play-by-play descriptions of the basketball games he'd watched that day, Jill thought how truly perfect the afternoon with Carrie had indeed been.

Carl, her father-in-law, looked at her once, his eyes questioning, but she smiled and turned her attention to Craig. She tried—she really did—to muster up some enthusiasm for what Craig loved. Unfortunately, it just wouldn't come.

CHAPTER FIFTEEN

"Five sunny days in a row," Carrie exclaimed one day weeks later. "Do you think spring is really here?"

Jill laughed. "March is barely here. I don't think you should lay claim to spring too."

"It feels like spring. It even smells like spring. And look how swollen the trees are," she said. "Everything will be budding out soon." She turned to Jill. "I can't wait for green."

"I know. And this would be a good weekend to start on your flowerbeds."

Carrie nodded. "Yes, it would." Then she grinned. "Are you sure you have to go?"

"As much as I would love to be with you, Craig and Angie would never forgive me if I missed the state tournament."

"Oh, I know. I was being selfish."

"No you weren't," Jill said as she reached over and squeezed

Carrie's hand. She wasn't surprised when Carrie's fingers closed over hers. They had been doing that a lot lately. Touching. "And if I could get out of it, I'd ask you for the whole weekend," she said quietly. "The lunch hours seem shorter and shorter."

"Yes. It's probably because the weather is nice and we're out here, not stuck inside, that makes the time race." She slowly let Jill's hand slip away before turning back to the lake. "But the state tournament is a big deal, right?"

"Yeah, it's a big deal. Once in a lifetime thing for most of these kids. And Craig about passes out from excitement just talking about it. I can't imagine what he'll do at the game."

"Well, believe it or not, Josh even made mention that Kline was going to State. And Aaron tells me they've painted up the windows at both stores in town."

"Yes, everyone is excited. Arlene bought us all matching T-shirts to wear at the games. I have this fear that she's going to hold up a sign saying we're the coach's family."

Carrie laughed. "I can tell how enthused you are."

"Don't think I haven't thought about staying behind, because I have. But I'm sure the wrath of the basketball gods would rain down upon me!"

"Oh, well. Maybe soon we can find a weekend."

"Maybe." Jill turned on the bench, waiting until Carrie looked at her. Her blue eyes looked bright in the sunshine. Jill couldn't decide which color she liked best, this or the pale blue she saw more often. "I . . . I really miss talking to you, Carrie. I mean, on the weekends." She paused. "I don't understand it," she admitted softly. "I've never had a friend like you. I've never *talked* to someone so much."

"I know exactly what you mean." Carrie sat up, resting her elbows on her thighs as she gazed out over the lake. "I don't know what it is about you but when you're around, everything seems so brilliant, so beautiful." She glanced at Jill quickly, then away. "I'm almost afraid of the colors I'll see this spring," she said with a laugh. "If you don't mind, I would love to paint you."

Jill smiled. "Paint me?"

"Yes. Not a portrait. I mean, outside, standing by the water, or sitting here on our bench, with the colors all bursting around you." She turned back to Jill. "What do you think?"

Jill tilted her head. "Will I get to keep it?"

"If you wish."

She nodded. "Yes. I would love for you to paint me."

CHAPTER SIXTEEN

In all the years she had known Craig, she'd never once seen him like this. But the silence was nearly unbearable. Unfortunately, she didn't know any inspiring sports quotes to cheer him up.

"It's really a nice evening. I think we should grill out," she said. "And I think we should ask your parents to join us. We owe them." She rolled her eyes. God, she must be desperate to want Arlene over here.

"I'm not really in the mood, babe."

She tucked her blond hair behind both ears and stood staring at him. His eyes were glued to the TV, a TV that stood dark and silent. Even his cell phone remained quiet.

"Craig, it *was* a good game," she said hesitantly.

"Good? We lost by one fucking point. You call that good?"

She raised her eyebrows. She hadn't heard him use the f-word in years. But she tried again.

"You went to State, Craig. You made it to the final game. You're acting like you got blown away."

"Blown away? We were picked to win. We *should* have won." He shook his head. "Goddamned call. It wasn't a foul. Jesus! Anybody could tell it wasn't a foul."

She sighed. "Okay, fine," she murmured. *I tried.*

She went through the kitchen and into the garage where they kept the freezer. She took out four steaks, then hesitated, finally tossing two back in. If he didn't want his parents over, she certainly wasn't going to invite them. She feared she would end up entertaining them while he sulked in private. But no, sulking is always better when you have an audience. So, she pulled out the other two steaks after all.

And after a call to Arlene to let her know the mood her son was in, she went about catching up on the laundry she'd missed while they were gone. When she walked through the house to go upstairs, Craig was still in the same position, staring at the TV. She knew it must be devastating to lose the championship game, but still, they'd at least made it that far. How many teams could say that? She opened her mouth to say those very words but stopped. What did she know about it?

She methodically unpacked their luggage and piled up their dirty clothes to take downstairs. And she thought she had time to shower before his parents would be there. She was about to go into Angie's room to retrieve her clothes when the door opened. Craig stood there, his face drawn, sullen.

She raised her eyebrows.

He shrugged then motioned to the bed. "I could use a little attention," he said.

"Attention?"

He walked closer. "Yeah." He took her hands and pulled her to him. "It's been weeks since we've made love."

Try months.

She stepped out of his embrace, holding him at arm's length. "You don't want to make love, Craig. You want to have sex."

"And? So?"

"And so I don't. Besides, your parents are coming over any minute."

"I told you I wasn't in the mood," he said loudly.

"Well they're coming over just the same. We're having steaks."

"I swear, Jill, can't we spend one night alone?"

She put her hands on her hips and glared at him. "Since January, you have been gone nearly every night of the week with basketball. Don't talk to me about spending time alone."

"It's my job, for Christ's sake. You know that."

"Oh yes, I know."

"And it's not like I didn't ask you to come with me. You just never want to."

"Well, like you said, it's *your* job."

"What's that supposed to mean?"

She turned around and gathered up an armload of dirty clothes. She shook her head. "It means nothing, Craig. But I don't care to join you in your pity party. You should be proud of how far you and the team went. These are *kids*, Craig. They look up to you. Is this what you want them to see?"

"You just don't understand," he said. "You never did. It's not just a *game*, Jill. It's about life."

"So the message you want to portray is that you lost the game, you lost at life? Give me a break. They're sixteen, seventeen years old. How sad is it if you make them believe that this weekend was the most important event in their young lives? They've got their whole life in front of them."

"Yeah, well I don't," he said angrily as he turned away.

"And it's always about you," she murmured. She closed her eyes, finally letting out her breath. He wasn't worried about the kids and their frame of mind, he was just concerned about himself. It was what made him a good coach—the fear of failing. It was also what made him a horrible coach.

Later, after steaks and after his mother had effectively consoled him, he was able to turn on his cell phone. It hadn't stopped ringing.

So as soon as Arlene and Carl left, she poured a glass of wine and retreated to the back deck. The nights were still cool but not unbearably cold. The sweatshirt she'd pulled on was plenty warm enough.

She sat down and put the swing in motion with her foot, enjoying the quiet finally after three days of basketball. She wasn't even going to allow Arlene's remarks about Angie make her feel guilty. Angie was at Shelly's. And yes, it *was* a school night. But *no*, she wasn't a horrible mother. Angie had called, asking if she could stay over. After talking to Shelly's mom to make sure it was okay with them, she said yes. Their evening of rented movies and pizza sounded more fun anyway.

She leaned her head back and closed her eyes, trying to relax after the whirlwind weekend they'd had. And as always, when she allowed them, thoughts of Carrie crept into her mind.

She'd intentionally kept her at bay, trying hard to blend in with the family, to enjoy the basketball weekend like the others were. Even at night, as she lay in bed, long after Craig had gone to sleep, she'd purposely shut her mind to any thoughts of Carrie.

But now back home, back in her familiar surroundings, alone in the quiet evening, she allowed them to come. And it wasn't difficult at all to conjure up Carrie's face, her smile, her salt-and-pepper hair that stood in all directions . . . and the pale blue eyes she'd grown to love.

Love?

She opened her eyes quickly, her heart pounding nervously in her chest. *Love?* She relaxed. Yes, love. Carrie was a friend. In fact, a good friend, a best friend, really. So that stood to reason she'd feel *something* for her. Surely.

So she closed her eyes again, again putting the swing in motion, knowing, thankfully, that tomorrow was Monday. She smiled as a familiar peace settled over her.

CHAPTER SEVENTEEN

Jill didn't know who was more surprised by the hug but she simply couldn't stop herself when Carrie walked out to the porch to meet her. Embarrassed, she pulled away, but Carrie kept a hold on her hand. Their eyes held for a long moment then Carrie finally grinned and released her.

"Miss me?"

Jill shrugged nonchalantly. "A little. Maybe."

"Sorry about the game."

"Not nearly as sorry as I am."

"Oh? He took it hard?"

"Like it was life or death," Jill said. "I can't tell you how glad I am it's over."

"Well, come inside. I made us sandwiches. And if the rain stays away, we can go down to the pier later. Or we can just stay inside the sunroom."

"The wind is a little cold today, isn't it?"

"Yeah, I guess my prediction of an early spring was wrong," Carrie said as she held the door to the sunroom open.

Jill squeezed her arm as she walked past. "Spring will be here before you know it." She stopped short when she walked into the sunroom. The small wicker table that sat in front of the garden loveseat was decorated with a colorful tablecloth, and a vase held half a dozen red roses. She turned slowly, finding Carrie's eyes.

"It's beautiful," she said quietly.

Carrie shrugged and Jill noticed the slight blush that crept upon her face. "Nothing fancy," she said. "I just bought the roses on a whim."

"It was . . . it was sweet of you," Jill said lightly. She walked closer, bending to inhale the fragrance. She straightened with a smile. "Wonderful."

"Well, sit . . . relax. I'll bring out lunch."

"I can help."

"No, no. I've got it."

Jill watched her hurry into the cottage then she moved to the loveseat, taking her normal position on the end. Without thinking, she bent again to sniff the roses.

"I'm glad you like them," Carrie said quietly behind her.

Jill turned, smiling before taking the tray from Carrie. It was laden with sandwiches on onion rolls, two large dill pickles, a small tray of potato chips and a bowl of fresh fruit. Carrie went back for the glasses of tea then joined Jill on the loveseat.

"You went to too much trouble," Jill accused.

"Absolutely not. The strawberries are in season, I couldn't resist."

"Well, everything looks lovely, thank you." She picked up her sandwich and took a bite, moaning slightly as she tasted the spicy banana peppers Carrie had taught her to like.

"Tell me about the weekend," Carrie coaxed as she popped a strawberry into her mouth.

Jill smiled. "I hate to admit it but I was secretly hoping we'd lose the first game. And there was not one thing relaxing about the weekend. We stayed in the same hotel where all the teams stayed. Imagine hundreds of high school kids roaming the halls."

Carrie gave an exaggerated shudder. "I try not to."

"And then there was the constant companionship of my mother-in-law. I swear I didn't have a moment to myself. Breakfast, lunch and dinner, the games—she was everywhere," Jill said with a laugh. "Of course, Craig rode on the bus with the team, so Angie and I had the pleasure of driving down and back with them. Which surprisingly wasn't the worst part."

"Which was?"

"Which was when Craig got home." But she shook her head. "Enough of that. Tell me what you did over the weekend."

"Oh, it was totally stress-free and a little boring," Carrie said as she put her sandwich down. "James was actually home at a decent hour Friday, so he took me and Aaron out to dinner. Josh was on a date," she said with a smile. "I came out here on Saturday because the weather was so nice. Josh took Aaron and a couple of his friends to the mall and the movies, so I was able to spend the whole day out here. I got most of Joshua's old flowerbed cleaned out."

"I can't wait to see it."

"And I can't wait to plant flowers," Carrie said.

"What about yesterday? What did you do?"

"Yesterday was one of the rare days where we were all actually home at the same time. I cooked a pot roast and we had a real family dinner," she said. "It was just a lazy day."

"Lazy days are nice."

"Yes." Carrie looked away, then back at Jill. "I . . . I missed you. This weekend, I missed you."

Jill nodded. "I missed you too," she said quietly. Blue eyes held hers and she didn't try to pull away. "I seem to miss you more and more," she murmured.

"Do you think about me?"

"Yes."

"I think about you too. I didn't understand it at first. Then when I finally did understand it, it scared the hell out of me."

Jill frowned. "What do you mean?"

Carrie shook her head. "What's more scary is wondering if you feel it too," she whispered.

Jill's heart pounded loudly in her chest and she forgot to breathe. She stared into the blue eyes that were so close, blue eyes she'd learned to read so well. The hammering of her pulse wasn't out of fear, she realized.

"Feel what?" she breathed.

"This. Feel this," Carrie whispered as she leaned closer.

Jill knew what was happening but she still couldn't stop it. Her eyes slipped closed when she felt Carrie's lips brush across her own. She gasped at the contact then moaned as Carrie's mouth returned. Her own lips parted, moving with Carrie's as the kiss deepened. Warning bells clamored to be heard and it was only the sound of her ragged breathing that brought her to her senses.

She pulled away abruptly, her eyes wide as her fingers touched her lips where Carrie's mouth had been.

"Oh my God," she whispered. She shook her head, finally standing, backing away. An immediate look of regret crossed Carrie's face.

"Jill, God, I'm so sorry. I don't know what came over me. I just . . . I misread you, I guess. I misread all of this," she said as she stood, walking closer.

Jill shook her head and moved farther away. *Misread her?*

"Your friendship means more to me than anything, Jill. Please, I'm so sorry. I'm just an idiot."

Jill backed up then headed quickly to the door, her eyes still wide. "I've got to go," she whispered.

"No, please don't go. I am so, so sorry. Please . . ."

Jill opened the door then stopped, turning around to face Carrie. Their eyes held and Jill could no longer deny what was so blatantly obvious. They'd been innocently touching for weeks.

"Yes," she whispered.

Carrie frowned. "Yes what?"

"Yes, I feel it too," Jill said quickly before she fled from the cottage.

I won't see her again.

But the thought brought pain akin to a physical blow. She wrapped both arms around herself and put the swing in motion. How could she not see her? Her body hadn't felt so alive in years—and all from the briefest of kisses from another woman.

A woman.

She closed her eyes. A woman. But not just any woman. Carrie. Carrie, who had become her closest friend, her confidant, her escape. Carrie, who had begun to creep into her thoughts when she shouldn't have.

How could she not see her?

And the kiss? What about the kiss?

Jill felt the unfamiliar fluttering of her heart at just the thought of them kissing. A tiny kiss but a kiss nonetheless. But what did it mean?

She closed her eyes again. *You know what it means. You know exactly what it means.*

Yes, she knew what it meant, she wasn't that naive. And if she saw her again, what? Would Carrie continue to apologize? Would they blow it off as temporary insanity? Or would they talk about it, discuss it, analyze it?

Or would they simply pretend it never happened?

No. How could they? The attraction that Jill was trying to hide from—run from—was staring her right in the face. An attraction she didn't know what to do with, an attraction that had been teetering on the edge of physical, of sexual, for weeks now.

Refusing to acknowledge it wasn't going to make it go away. But accepting it wasn't something Jill thought she was prepared to do.

Because if she accepted it, her life would never be the same.

CHAPTER EIGHTEEN

On days like today, Jill was happy to have an assistant. Work she normally did herself, work she could do in her sleep, was but a jumbled mess. She couldn't concentrate on anything, much less numbers. So, she lied. On the pretense of working on their new radio ad, she shoved the week's receivables off on Harriet. The initial guilt she felt disappeared quickly as Harriet's eyes brightened at the prospect of doing something other than the mundane chores of an office assistant.

So, with her door closed, Jill pulled up the radio ad, not bothering to read through the thirty-second spot. It was just scrambled words on the page, much like the numbers had been.

She couldn't get her mind focused on anything.

Anything but Carrie, that is.

And she had no idea what she was going to do. She didn't know what to do with Craig, her marriage, and she certainly didn't know what to do about Carrie, about her feelings for the other woman.

She spun her chair around, staring out the window, watching the light rain splatter against the glass. Last night, after Craig's halfhearted attempt to make love was met with resistance, he'd wanted to talk about it. It had finally dawned on him that it had been months since they'd touched. She couldn't deal with his questions and she almost gave in and had sex with him, but in the end, she couldn't.

"Are you going to tell me what's going on or what?"

"There's nothing going on, Craig."

"So if it's not another man, what? You just all of a sudden decided you don't want to have sex with me?"

She got out of bed and paced slowly across the room. "Not all of a sudden," she said. "You're hardly ever home, Craig. And when you are home, you're on your cell." She held her hands out and shrugged. "It's like I'm invisible."

"What are you talking about? You're not invisible."

"I feel invisible. I do your laundry, I cook your meals, I keep your house. Same with Angie. I feel like your maid service."

"Oh, now you're talking crazy. I don't treat you like my maid. But babe, coaching takes a lot of time. You know that."

"Yes, I know that, Craig. But I feel like we're nearly strangers. So forgive me if I don't get all excited about having sex with you."

She sighed. His answer to that was to childishly stomp into the spare room to sleep, leaving her alone for the rest of the night, alone with her thoughts. And she finally went to sleep after coming to the conclusion that she would not see Carrie anymore. She didn't think her marriage could survive it if she did.

But in the light of day, when she woke up alone, the only thing on her mind was Carrie. Not her marriage, not her husband. Just Carrie and the brief kiss they'd shared.

And now, as she watched the rain, she had no earthly idea what she was going to do.

At ten minutes to one, as she paced nervously back and forth in the office—still trying to decide if she was going to see Carrie or not, and if she did, wondering what in the world she was going to say to her—her cell rang. She actually trembled when she saw the name displayed and she held the phone to her chest for a few seconds before answering.

Quiet breathing was all she heard, then a subtle clearing of the throat.

"Please come to lunch."

As she gripped the phone tightly, eyes squeezed shut, she nodded. "Yes," she said quietly.

"I'm sorry, Jill. I don't know what else to say."

It was Jill's turn to pause and she opened her eyes, feeling comforted for the first time that day by the quiet rain that fell. "It's raining," she murmured.

"Yes."

"Do you think I bring the rain?" Jill closed her eyes again. She could picture Carrie's face, could see the smile that tugged at her lips.

"I love the rain, Jill."

Jill nodded. "I'll see you in a bit."

And a few minutes later, when she saw Harriet pull into her parking space, Jill sprinted out the door with only a wave in Harriet's direction. She didn't think about what was going to happen at lunch, she didn't think about what they were going to say to one another. It didn't matter. She only knew she had to see Carrie, had to be with her. The pull was too strong.

But that didn't stop the nervousness she felt as she stood out in the rain, hesitating before going to the door. As she walked around the back, she saw her, standing in the sunroom, the door to the cottage open, inviting. Their eyes collided, the glass windows doing nothing to curb the intensity of their glance.

She finally brushed at the water droplets running down her face and realized she was getting soaked. She moved, walking to the door, pausing again before opening it.

Carrie stayed where she was, her eyes never leaving Jill's.

"I'm sorry," she said. "I never—"

"Please don't say you're sorry again," Jill said. She walked closer then stopped. She looked away for a moment, then back to Carrie. "When . . . when's the last time you slept with your husband?" she asked quietly.

Carrie looked startled by the question.

"When?" Jill whispered.

"It's been a long time."

"When?" Jill asked again.

"Probably . . . I don't know, December maybe. Before Christmas."

Jill closed her eyes, nodding. "I've . . . I've not had sex with Craig since I met you." She opened her eyes again, finding Carrie there.

"Why do you think that is?" Carrie asked.

"We know why. Don't we?"

Carrie nodded. "Yes, we know."

"But Carrie, I'm not—"

"I know."

"Then why do I want you to kiss me again? I mean, I know all of the reasons why we shouldn't. That doesn't change anything though, does it? I still want you to kiss me."

Carrie hesitated then smiled. "You're soaking wet. Let me get you a towel."

Jill grabbed her arm as Carrie turned. "You want to just avoid it? You kiss me then you want to pretend it didn't happen?"

"I can't pretend it didn't happen, Jill. I've thought of little else since then. But if I don't leave and do something—like get you a towel—then I'm going to kiss you again. And then we will definitely have a problem."

It was an out. Jill could let her go, could let her escape into the cottage. They could avoid the subject, they could even have lunch. But Jill's grip tightened on Carrie's arm. She didn't want to let her go.

"Kiss me again," she whispered.

But Carrie shook her head. "No. No, I won't be the one." She stepped away, arms at her sides.

"I want . . . I want you to kiss me," Jill said again.

Carrie tilted her head, her eyes looking into Jill's very soul. "Then come kiss me," she whispered.

It was a command Jill couldn't resist. She took a step closer, feeling the electricity in the room, seeing the anticipation in Carrie's eyes. She was surprised at the pulse that beat rapidly at Carrie's throat, surprised at the difficulty she had breathing, surprised at the *need* she had to kiss Carrie.

She felt Carrie tremble as she slid her hands up Carrie's arms. Then her own hand shook as she reached up, her fingers lightly touching Carrie's face. She dropped her gaze from Carrie's eyes to her lips, watching in fascination as they parted, watching as Carrie's tongue came out to wet them. The tightening in her chest and the breath she couldn't take told her all she needed to know. She would surely *die* if she didn't kiss her.

But in the end, it was Carrie who closed the space between them, Carrie whose lips claimed hers with such urgency, such *passion*, that Jill felt her knees quake from it all.

Her eyes slammed shut as she moaned, her mouth opening as she clutched Carrie's shoulders. The tongue that shyly, slowly met hers drove out all rational thought. She felt Carrie's arms slip around her, let herself be pulled flush into her embrace. A feeling like none she'd never experienced before took hold of her and she let it have full rein. There was to be no denying it.

That's why—when Carrie stepped away, when they stood

there both breathing heavily, when Carrie tugged on her hand and led her into the cottage—she didn't try to stop, she didn't try to pull away.

Because there was no denying it.

She stood there silently, the drapes causing shadows to dance upon the bed. There was no hesitation, no apprehension . . . there was only nervousness she couldn't quell. But when Carrie unbuttoned her blouse, exposing her lacy bra . . . when Jill saw those blue eyes darken with desire, even the nervousness left her. She let her blouse fall to the floor, unconcerned with its fate. The wool slacks she'd donned that morning slid smoothly down her legs. But when Carrie's hands reached for her bra, Jill stopped them.

"Take it off," Jill whispered, tugging at the bulky sweater Carrie wore. Her breath caught as Carrie pulled the sweater over her head. She wore no bra. Her breasts were small, her nipples hardening quickly as Jill stared. She finally raised her eyes to Carrie. "We're going to make love."

Carrie nodded. "Yes, we're going to make love."

Her hands were sure as she reached out to touch Carrie. The skin was soft under her fingers, soft and smooth, and she realized she had dreamed of this moment since the day she'd first looked into Carrie's eyes.

She wasn't afraid when Carrie guided her to the bed, wasn't afraid when she pulled Carrie to her. Instinctively, her hands moved across skin, knowing where to touch, how to touch.

But when Carrie's hands spread her thighs, when Carrie settled between her legs, Jill wasn't prepared for the way her body reacted to her touch. Her hips rose, melding with Carrie's, and she felt a flood of wetness soak her. Then Carrie's mouth was there, silencing her moan, taking the breath from her. But then that mouth pulled away, moving lower.

Jill shuddered when soft lips covered her breast, when a warm tongue raked across her nipple. Her body pulsed, moving wildly against Carrie's. She ran her fingers through Carrie's short hair, holding her tightly against her breast. Then a hand moved between their bodies and she felt Carrie shift, felt that hand slide over her hip.

She wasn't certain what she expected to feel when Carrie touched her, but the jolt of desire that pierced her soul was not it. Fingers slipped into her wetness and she cried out, her head tilted back, eyes slammed shut as Carrie entered her. Her hips jerked, taking Carrie inside, moving with each stroke of her fingers.

Then she felt Carrie move, felt Carrie's wetness as Carrie straddled her thigh. Blindly, she reached her hand out, wanting to touch Carrie, wanting to feel her. But the instant her hand moved between their bodies, the instant her fingers felt Carrie's wetness as Carrie slammed down on them, the instant she *touched* Carrie, she climaxed with such wild abandon her throat ached from the scream she tried to contain. Her body nearly convulsed as she came but she was coherent enough to feel Carrie's orgasm, coherent enough to feel her fingers enveloped by Carrie's wetness, coherent enough to hear her name leave Carrie's lips as she came.

Coherent enough to know what they'd just done.

CHAPTER NINETEEN

She filled the wineglass for the third time, noting absently that the bottle was nearly empty. Numbly she set it aside, moving slowly along the deck, staying out of the drizzle that had been falling all day.

Craig was not home and she had no idea where he was. Angie was up in her room doing homework. And Jill paced nervously on the deck, her mind racing, thousands of thoughts crowding in as she tried to determine how she felt. It stood to reason she should feel guilty. After all, she'd just been intimate with someone other than her husband.

But surprisingly, she was able to push the guilt away. What they'd shared today was inevitable. Jill couldn't have stopped it any sooner than she could have stopped a speeding train. She knew when she went there what would happen. She knew it in her heart . . . she knew it in her soul.

But what it all meant, she had no idea. There hadn't been time to talk, time to savor their intimacy. Carrie had asked her to call in, had asked her to stay the afternoon with her but Jill couldn't think of an excuse to give Harriet.

So in the end, she'd fled, her blouse and suit jacket a wrinkled mess, a testament as to how she'd spent her lunch hour. As it was, she was twenty minutes late but Harriet didn't comment. She simply raised her eyebrows as Jill hurried into the ladies' room. And she nearly cried when she saw her reflection in the mirror. Hardly a hint of makeup remained and her lips, still swollen from their lovemaking, were unnaturally red.

She looked frightful.

And it was just a blessing she didn't have to face Craig because she had no idea how she would react when she saw him, no idea what her eyes would reveal. Would he know? Would he suspect? And the next time he kissed her, would she pull away, would she shy away from his touch?

His touch. How could she ever allow him to touch her after what she'd just shared with Carrie? Carrie's touch couldn't have been more different than Craig's, yet her hands upon her skin made her body come alive, made it tingle with want, with need. It was like Carrie knew exactly how to touch her, when to touch her . . . *where* to touch her.

She paused, the wineglass nearly to her lips but she lowered it again. Yes, Carrie knew how to touch her. Carrie knew *exactly* how to touch her.

"Oh my God," she whispered.

She's been with a woman before.

CHAPTER TWENTY

Jill sat in her car for a long moment, actually nervous about seeing Carrie. She wasn't sure what to expect. She didn't know how she would react, she didn't know how Carrie would react. Would they hug? Would they kiss? Would they have lunch like normal?

Or would they make love again?

Jill closed her eyes, aware of the trembling of her body at just the thought. Is that what she wanted? To make love again? To touch Carrie? To have Carrie touch her? Was this the start of an affair . . . an affair with another woman? Or was it a one-time thing? A one-time lapse in judgment?

She shook her head. She didn't know what it was, not yet. But she did know it was not a one-time thing. Her body told her that. So she opened the door and got out, the rain that had lingered overnight and into the morning had dissipated, giving way to colder temperatures but clearing skies.

The low heels she'd slipped on that morning clicked loudly on the driveway as she hurried around back to the sunporch. As expected, Carrie was standing inside waiting. And as before, Jill stopped, her eyes colliding with Carrie's through the windows. Again, she didn't know what she expected, but not this rapid hammering of her heart and weak knees. Only when Carrie gave her a hesitant smile was she able to walk in, pausing to wipe her feet on the rug before going into the sunroom.

They stood there, several feet apart, both staring, both silent. Finally, Carrie tilted her head, eyebrows raised.

"Are you sorry?" she asked quietly.

Jill shook her head. "No." Then, "Are you?"

"No, not . . . not at all."

Jill nodded, her hands clutched together nervously in front of her. She finally asked the one question that had been haunting her all night, all morning.

"You've been with a woman before, haven't you?"

Carrie was obviously startled by the question and she drew her brows together.

"Why do you say that?"

Jill met her eyes, holding them. "Because when you touched me, it was . . . it was a familiar touch."

Carrie let out her breath then slowly nodded. "Yes."

Jill didn't know what to say, didn't know what to make of the sharp pain that pierced her soul. For some reason, she wanted the answer to be no.

"Come inside. Let's talk. I'll tell you about it."

Jill wasn't sure she wanted to know the details, wasn't sure she could handle it. What if it was someone like her? Someone just drifting along in her marriage, someone looking for something more in life, something more in a relationship?

"Jill?"

Jill looked up, nodded and followed Carrie into the cottage, followed her to the tiny loveseat in the sitting area. But before she could sit, Carrie took her hands, pulling her close. Jill closed her eyes, moving into the embrace, letting her arms slide around Carrie's waist, letting her body reconnect with Carrie's.

"I was afraid you weren't going to come today," Carrie whispered into her ear.

Jill shook her head then slowly pulled away, meeting Carrie's eyes. The desire she remembered from yesterday was still there.

"Kiss me," she murmured, closing her eyes again as Carrie's lips moved lightly, softly against her own. She moaned, all the emotion, all the excitement returning at her kiss. Her mouth opened, wanting more, but Carrie pulled away.

"We should talk," she said, her breath coming as fast as Jill's.

Jill stepped out of her embrace, embarrassed by her desire. "Yes, okay. You're right."

Carrie walked into the kitchen, picking up the two glasses she'd filled with water earlier. She handed one to Jill, then joined her on the loveseat. Jill reached out and took her hand, letting their fingers entwine.

"Tell me."

Carrie nodded and cleared her throat. Jill was surprised at her own nervousness, her apprehension as to what Carrie would say.

"I can imagine what you're thinking," Carrie said, smiling at the look of embarrassment on Jill's face. "But it was a long, long time ago. In college," she said. "I had just met James, had just started dating him. We went to this party, our first party together. And there was this girl there, she was a few years older than me, a senior," she said. "Anyway, she flirted shamelessly with me. Before the end of the night, she'd managed to steal a kiss and walk away with my phone number." Carrie met Jill's eyes, holding them. "And two nights later, I slept with her."

"But James?"

"I didn't quite know what to do with James and I certainly didn't know what to do with her. She was just so exciting, so different. But three weeks later, after being with her nearly every night, she up and left. Quit school and took a job in Los Angeles, just like that. She barely said good-bye. And I was devastated." She shrugged. "And James was still there, still wanting to date me. I convinced myself I had temporary insanity and went on to pretend the whole affair never happened."

"And James never knew?"

"No. But we weren't sleeping together. It was a long time before I could sleep with him."

"And . . . and no one since then?" Jill asked quietly.

"No. Honestly, the thought never even crossed my mind. Not until I met you," Carrie said. She squeezed hard on Jill's hand then brought it up to her lips. "And once I realized what it was I felt for you, I couldn't stop thinking about it. It was like I was going to die if I didn't touch you."

Jill slowly shook her head, her eyes staring at the lips that had just brushed against her palm.

"I don't . . . I don't know what to say."

"Tell me how you *feel*, Jill. Tell me if you feel guilty for what we did. I'll understand. Tell me if you don't ever want to . . . to make love again," she whispered. "I'll understand that too. Just tell me. Don't let me sit here and speculate, like I've been doing since you left yesterday."

"No, no, I'm sorry. But I'm not certain how I feel. I should feel guilty, shouldn't I? But I don't. Not really." She caught her breath. "The thought of not seeing you again, not being with you again . . . it's not an option." She held Carrie's eyes. "Is it?"

CHAPTER TWENTY-ONE

Jill looked up as the kitchen door opened, surprised to find Arlene in the doorway. She closed the lid on the pot as she glanced at her mother-in-law, wondering at her unannounced visit.

"Hello," Jill said. "Usually it's only Angie and Craig who don't bother to knock when they come in that door," she said, unable to keep the sarcasm out of her voice.

Arlene ignored her comment as she walked into the room. "Dinner?"

Jill nodded. "Soup."

"To hear Angie tell it, you seldom cook dinner."

Jill frowned. "I cook dinner every night. Well, every night that someone's here to eat it." She moved away. "Which is not often," she added.

"Yes, well, I'm wondering if you have a minute to visit,"

Arlene said.

"Visit?"

"Yes. I'm worried about you. About you and Craig."

"What in the world for?"

Arlene clasped her hands together then released them. She shook her head slowly before answering.

"He tells me something's wrong. He says it's been . . . well, it's been awhile since you've . . . well, since you've been intimate. I know that part of your marriage is none of my business but—"

"You're right. It's none of your business," Jill said as she walked to the door. She held it open. "It's absolutely none of your business."

"My son is my business."

"Well my sex life is not."

"Jill, you're like a daughter to me, you know that, right?"

Jill barely resisted the urge to roll her eyes. She could not, however, resist a sarcastic laugh. "Sure, Arlene."

"Of course you are. And if you're having some issues now, some problems, I'm here for you."

"Issues?"

Arlene took a step closer, her voice low. "If you're seeing another man, it's only fair that you let Craig know."

Jill took a deep breath, hating the fact that her heart was pounding nervously. "Arlene, as you said, this is none of your business. But rest assured, there's not another man involved."

"Then what is it?"

Jill glanced to the ceiling then closed her eyes. "I'm not having this discussion with you. If Craig has questions, he can ask me. But I refuse to go through you." She opened the door wider. "Now, if there's nothing else."

Arlene walked past her to leave but paused at the door. "You best be careful," she said quietly. "A man like Craig may find he's wanted elsewhere. What you won't give him, someone else will."

She turned and walked away before Jill could reply. She stood there, watching her mother-in-law as she moved down the driveway. She finally went back into the kitchen, lifting the lid and stirring the soup without thought, wondering what in the world she was going to do.

She couldn't go on like this for long. Craig would demand answers. Answers she wasn't prepared to give.

In fact, she and Carrie hadn't spoken at all about their lives, their husbands, their families. What in the world were they going to do?

CHAPTER TWENTY-TWO

Jill lay still, lazily watching Carrie's hand as it moved across her skin, inching closer and closer to her breast. Her eyes slid closed when it reached its destination, a smile forming as she felt Carrie's thumb lightly rub across her nipple.

"Your skin is so soft," Carrie whispered, her mouth replacing her fingers upon her breast.

"God, I love when you do that," Jill breathed, her chest arching against Carrie's mouth. Such an intimate, gentle gesture, something she was not used to in her marriage.

"I love the way you taste," Carrie said as her lips moved across her skin.

Jill spread her thighs, her hands at Carrie's hips gathering her close again. They didn't have time, yet Jill couldn't deny her body, couldn't forsake her desire just because the clock ticked closer and closer to two.

But Carrie's hands stilled, her mouth left Jill's breast, returning once to place the briefest of kisses there.

"It's time," she whispered.

Jill groaned, searching for Carrie's hand, pulling it quickly between her legs, holding it there. She arched against it, loving the feeling of Carrie's fingers as they entered her.

"We've got to have a Saturday," Carrie said against her lips. "I could spend hours loving you."

Jill lay still, letting Carrie's fingers slip from her, knowing they didn't have time. She rolled to her side, resting her head on her hand, watching Carrie, waiting for the pale blue eyes to travel over her body, pausing at her breasts before meeting her own.

"You're so incredibly beautiful," Carrie whispered.

"You make me feel beautiful."

As if she couldn't stop it, Carrie's hand moved, softly touching Jill's breast, watching as her nipples hardened from her touch.

"Isn't it amazing how much life we can cram into an hour every day? Then the weekend comes and I die a little each day I don't see you."

"I know. What about Saturday after next?"

"Can you get away?"

"There's a baseball tournament. Angie is going too. Apparently some boy on the team is really hot," she said with a laugh.

"So we could spend the day together?"

"Yes, the whole day."

CHAPTER TWENTY-THREE

Jill noticed the nights were getting warmer as she walked silently across the deck and slipped onto the swing. Most of the trees had already budded out, obscuring the night sky. She smiled, remembering Carrie's excitement at lunch as they sat at the pier, the sunshine warm upon them. The green was returning and Carrie talked animatedly about all the different things she wanted to paint.

"I want to do you in the flower garden and right here on the pier."

Jill had laughed. "Do me, huh?"

Carrie smiled wickedly. "Yes, do you in watercolors."

Jill put the swing in motion and her thoughts, as always, lingered on the other woman. It scared her to admit it but she knew she was falling in love with her. And she didn't have a clue as to what she was going to do about it. They were just so connected on every level, it was as if their souls had called out to each other, not resting until they were joined.

But they were both married, both with children. What were they going to do? How long could they continue this affair?

How long could she go before Craig demanded answers, demanded she be a wife to him in all ways? How long could she avoid him?

Because that was one thing she was sure of. She could endure sharing his bed, she could even endure the chaste good night kiss on the few occasions they actually went to bed at the same time, but she could not—would not—endure his touch.

And eventually he would demand it. Oh, she could put him off for awhile. It was baseball season. He had an activity to keep him occupied. But in little more than a month, school would be over with and summer would be upon them. And he would be home more unless she convinced him to join a fourth softball team.

She sighed and sipped from her glass of wine. It was becoming too much to think about. So she pushed all of it aside and closed her eyes, remembering Carrie's touch upon her skin instead, her lips upon her breasts, her hands as they parted her thighs.

Oh my.

She took a deep breath, still amazed that the touch of another woman could bring her to such heights, could bring her such complete satisfaction. And amazed that her own touch had the power to make Carrie tremble in her arms, make Carrie beg for release, make Carrie scream her name.

"Babe?"

Jill jumped, nearly dropping her wineglass. She was so lost in her thoughts, she never heard Craig come home.

"Sorry, I didn't mean to scare you," he said. "Thought you heard me."

"No. I was . . . I was far away, I guess. What are you doing home already?"

"It's nine thirty."

Her eyes widened. "I had no idea it was that late. Did Angie ride with you?"

"Yeah. She's upstairs already." He walked closer, finally sitting down on the swing beside her. "Do you feel like talking?"

She wondered if she said no, would he leave it at that. But she nodded. "Sure."

"I know my mother came over the other week. I just want you to know I didn't ask her to do that."

"It's none of her business."

"I know. But I've always been able to talk to her about stuff, this was no different." He shrugged. "You say it's not another man, and I want to believe you, but it's the only explanation we can come up with."

"We? You and your mother?"

"Yes." He stood up and walked to the edge of the deck. "Please, Jill, just tell me. This speculating about who he is just makes me crazy."

"I'm not seeing another man, Craig. I don't know what's going on with me, I really don't. I only know I don't have the . . . the *desire* to sleep with you, to be intimate with you. I'm sorry. I don't know what else you want me to say."

He nodded. "Then maybe we need to see someone."

"See someone?"

"A marriage counselor."

"Arlene wants us to see a marriage counselor?"

"It couldn't hurt."

"It couldn't help."

"Why not? Why won't you even try?"

Jill stared at him. "What makes you think I've not been trying? All these years, what makes you think I've not tried?"

"So now what? We go on like this until you say you want a divorce?"

"What do you want, Craig?"

"I want our life back," he said loudly.

"What life is that? Where you're gone four or five nights a week and I'm here, tending to the house and laundry, doing your shopping and cleaning. And on the few occasions where we're actually home and awake at the same time, I'm in your bed so you can have sex. Is that the life you're talking about?"

"Is that . . . is that your version of our life?" he asked quietly.

"Yes. Do you see it differently?"

"I'm a coach. I have obligations. You know that. Other wives understand."

"Name one other coach at Kline who is as involved in three sports as you are. And then find one who is on three softball teams during the summer."

"Oh, now you're bringing up my one leisure activity? Softball is the only time I get to relax. You think coaching is a piece of cake?"

"No, I know it's not. Obviously it takes up most of your time."

"What do you want me to do? You want me to quit coaching?"

"Craig, you love coaching more than anything in this world. More than me, more than Angie, more than our marriage. How can I possibly ask you to give it up? It's what makes you who you are."

He shook his head but didn't attempt to deny it. "So what do you want me to do?"

"I have no idea, Craig. You can be patient with me and see what happens, you can say the hell with it and file for divorce, I don't know."

"I don't want a divorce, Jill."

She shrugged. "Then I guess we'll go on and see what happens."

"Do you want me to move into the spare room?"

107

"Is that what you want to do?"

He shook his head. "Not really, no."

"Then don't."

She let out a heavy breath as he walked back into the house, feeling somewhat relieved that they'd talked but still wondering what she was going to do about her life. It wasn't fair to Craig to go on like they were if she had no intention of being his wife again.

And as the weeks went by, she realized how likely that was. The more time she spent with Carrie, the more time she wanted. Yet she didn't dare to dream they might have a life together. Carrie had her own family, her own husband.

CHAPTER TWENTY-FOUR

"Hey, Mom."

Jill glanced up from the paper then looked at the clock with a frown. "What in the world are you doing up already?"

"I'm going to the baseball tournament," Angie said.

"I thought you weren't leaving until nine."

"Shelly's dad is taking us instead. He wants to leave by eight."

"You need me to run you over there?"

"No, they're coming by."

"Okay." She pointed to the counter where the toaster sat. "You want some toast?"

Angie reached for a banana instead as she pulled out a chair. Jill watched her, wondering what was going on. Angie *never* sat down at the breakfast table with her.

"Mom, can I ask you something?"

Jill folded the paper and nodded. "Of course."

Angie tossed the banana nervously between her hands for a second, then took a quick breath. "Are you and Dad fighting?"

"Fighting?"

She looked away. "Are you going to get a divorce?"

"Why would you think that?"

"Grandma says you don't like Dad anymore."

"Grandma says that, huh? Well, I like your dad just fine."

"Do you still love him?"

Jill nodded. "Yes, I love him."

"Then what's wrong?"

"Angie, there's a difference between loving someone and being in love with them." Jill leaned closer. "You live here, Angie. You can see how it is. How little time we spend together. You can't sustain a marriage when you're never together."

"But that's your choice," Angie stated loudly. "You're the one who won't come to the games, you're the one who wants to stay here alone."

"Angie, going to the games is not something I want to do. I don't enjoy them."

"But why?"

"I just don't. That's your dad's job. I have a job too. And when I get off work at five, I don't want to have to go to your dad's job. Do you understand? It would be like me asking him to come to my work, to follow me out to construction sites on payday, or to sit around the office and watch me work."

"But that's not the same."

"Why not? Just because it's a game?" Jill shook her head. "When I get off of work, I want to come home. I don't want to go to a second job."

Angie stared at her and nodded. "I think I understand now. When you come home, there's nobody here."

"Exactly."

She shrugged. "So? Does that mean you're going to get a divorce?"

Jill sighed. "No. We're just working through some things now, Angie."

"Grandma says you're having an affair," Angie said quietly.

Jill smiled. "Grandma doesn't always know everything. She *thinks* she does but she doesn't."

Angie stood and nodded, seemingly satisfied with their conversation. But Jill's smile faded as soon as Angie slipped from the room. Was she having an affair? No. It felt too bright and fresh, too *joyous* to be an affair.

But if it wasn't an affair, then what was it? How long could she continue to lie to her family? How long could she continue to hide this new love she was feeling?

CHAPTER TWENTY-FIVE

It was with a satisfied push of the button that Jill closed the gate behind her. Closed the gate and closed out the world, if only for a day. But a whole day at that.

She parked beside Carrie's van, unable to contain the quiet laugh as she stepped out into the sunshine, nearly giddy with the prospect of spending the day with Carrie. Angie had been barely out the door when Jill grabbed the bag she'd packed the night before. A bag stuffed with a change of clothes, two bottles of wine, her gardening gloves and a denim baseball cap Craig rarely wore. For the last several weeks, Carrie had been adding flowers to the gardens but this was the first opportunity Jill would have to play in the dirt with her.

"When you said early, you weren't lying."

Jill turned, finding Carrie walking up from the pier, hands already muddy from the garden.

"You started without me," Jill accused.

"No, no. Planting is your chore today. I just brought the flowers down there then yanked a few weeds."

Jill laughed. "You can always be in charge of the weeds."

Carrie pointed down the winding road. "The gate?"

Jill nodded. "Closed and locked."

"Wonderful. Then the day is ours." Carrie led the way into the cottage, pausing to brush the dirt off her hands before going inside. "I took a chance you wouldn't want breakfast," she said. "But I made up some homemade chicken salad and picked up fresh sandwich rolls at the bakery." She stopped and smiled. "Oh, and I got some of that cheese you like. Did you remember the wine?"

Jill held up her bag. "Two bottles."

Carrie laughed. "Two? Are we going to make a day of it?"

Jill walked closer and leaned forward, lightly kissing Carrie on the lips. "We're going to make a good day of it."

"Yeah, we are. And after you've had your fun playing in the dirt, we're going to go fishing."

"Fishing? Like in a canoe?"

"I was thinking more off the pier. After we've had a bottle of wine, I'm not sure we should attempt a canoe lesson."

Jill put the two wine bottles on the bar then tossed her bag on the loveseat after pulling out her gardening gloves.

"Can I go down?" she asked, her eyes bright.

Carrie smiled. "I'll be right behind you. I've made some iced tea. I'll bring out a couple of glasses."

Jill stepped out into the sunshine and looked skyward, closing her eyes for a moment of quiet reflection, conscious of the peacefulness she felt being here. It was indeed as if they'd locked the world away.

"My mother used to call that woolgathering," Carrie said quietly from behind her.

Jill turned, finding Carrie's eyes. "Just thinking how nice it feels to be here."

Carrie nodded, her head tilted slightly. Then she raised an eyebrow. "Everything okay?"

"Oh, sure," Jill said quickly as she averted her eyes. Then she looked back at Carrie, finding the same gentle look in her face as always. "Just . . . a lot of questions at home," she finally said.

"I see. Well, let's go down to the pier. We'll talk," she said as she walked down the path.

Jill took one of the glasses of tea and waved her gloves in the air again. "I have flowers calling my name," she reminded her.

"Then we'll talk as we plant."

And they did, talking about everything under the sun before Carrie finally broached the subject of Jill's home life.

"It's one thing for Craig to want to discuss our marriage, quite another when my daughter does," Jill said. She took her gloves off and wiped her forehead before sitting down cross-legged on the ground. She absently brushed at the dirt clinging to her knees. "Arlene suggested to Craig that we need to see a marriage counselor." Jill leaned forward. "Craig tells her everything. I think it's just creepy for a son to discuss his sex life with his mother."

Carrie nodded but said nothing.

"We—me and Craig—had a talk," Jill said quietly. "He's . . . well, he thinks I'm having an affair."

Carrie tilted her head. "Aren't you?"

Jill slowly shook her head. "No. This doesn't feel like an affair to me."

Carrie let out her breath, a slight smile on her face. "Thank you," she whispered.

"But I don't know what to do," Jill said. "I can't . . . the thought of him touching me is nearly repulsive."

"I didn't want to know if you were sleeping with him," Carrie admitted. "I couldn't stand the thought, actually."

Jill looked away. "You've never really said . . . I mean, about

114

James," Jill said.

Carrie shook her head. "I've not had sex with him, no. In fact, I doubt he's even noticed."

"What do you mean?"

Carrie stood, brushing the dirt from her jeans before answering. "James is a classic workaholic. He has very little down time. He sleeps only four to five hours a night." She shrugged. "It hasn't been an issue."

When Jill would have spoken, Carrie held up her hand. "I'm ready to trade this tea in for wine. What do you say?"

"Excellent."

"Good. Then let's have an early lunch." Carrie pointed at the weathered picnic table. "You want to eat out here or in the cottage?"

Jill laughed. "I want to be outside as much as you do."

After they washed up, they hauled their lunch down to the pier in a huge picnic basket, wineglasses and all. Carrie tossed a blue cloth across the picnic table and Jill opened the wine.

For the next hour, they sat in the sun trading stories, leisurely munching on chicken salad sandwiches, cheese and fruit and fighting over the last of the wine.

"Do you realize how thoroughly I enjoy your company?" Carrie said as she set the empty wine bottle aside.

Jill reached across the table and squeezed her hand. "Yes," she said without question.

Carrie laughed.

"I didn't mean that to sound quite so conceited," Jill said. "I feel absolutely the same way." She twisted her napkin between her fingers, finally looking up, meeting Carrie's eyes. "You know, we can talk about anything, everything. We do talk about *everything*," she said. "Except us. We never talk about us."

Carrie held her eyes for a moment then looked away. "That's because I'm afraid of the answers."

"What do you mean?"

"We want more time together but there is no more time. We both have husbands, kids."

Jill cleared her throat, again twisting her napkin nervously. "How long can we do this?" She looked up into the clear sky above. "How long can I go on pretending to have a marriage when I just want to be with you?"

"Don't you think I feel the same? But you have a fourteen-year-old daughter whose relationship with you is tenuous at best. Are you willing to lose her?" Carrie took her hand, rubbing lightly against the palm. "My boys . . . it's different," she said. "They're older, for one thing. And Josh, well, Josh is my son. And Aaron worships the ground his father walks on. I'm sure their loyalties would lie there as well. And James, well, James has been too busy to notice anything out of the ordinary. He would be completely blown away, yes. But it's not me I'm worried about. It's you, Jill."

"I know. Angie would never forgive me, would never understand. Craig would be devastated." She squeezed Carrie's hand. "But I'm not sure how much weight all of that holds. I'm miserable at home. And they both know it, they just don't know why."

Carrie leaned her elbows on the table and rested her chin in her hands, staring at Jill. "At night when I'm in bed, you have no idea how much I long for it to be you beside me. I long to sleep with you, to wake up with you." She leaned back again and idly twirled her empty wineglass. "But we're not afforded that luxury."

Jill stared at the woman who had become so important to her, wondering what thoughts were racing through her mind. Dare she bring up the one word that had not been uttered? After knowing each other barely five months, dare she mention divorce? Was she ready to sever her ties with Craig? Was she ready to cause a rift with Angie? But perhaps she was premature. Had divorce even crossed Carrie's mind? Jill stared, waiting for the pale blue eyes to look up, waiting for them to look into her very soul.

And they did. And as always—when those eyes held her—she was convinced she'd stared into them many lifetimes ago.

Carrie finally smiled, releasing her. "I think I threatened you with fishing, didn't I?"

Jill relaxed, sensing Carrie had tired of their talk. So she let it go with a wave of her hand. "And threatened is the appropriate word," Jill agreed.

"By the middle of summer, I'll have you begging to go fishing. And in the canoe, no less." Carrie stood and motioned to the table. "If you'll pack all this back into the basket, I'll go get the fishing poles and worms."

Jill's eyes widened. "Worms?"

Carrie just grinned as she walked back toward the garage. Jill cleaned up from their lunch, her mind still locked on a dirty, wiggly worm.

"Surely she doesn't expect me to *touch* them," she muttered.

"It's just a worm," Carrie said patiently.

Jill shook her head. "Not doing it."

"Why not?"

"Well, gross and disgusting come to mind."

"I suppose if you catch a fish you'll want me to take it off of the hook for you too?"

"Trust me, I will not catch a fish."

"Don't be so sure. I always catch fish here off the pier," Carrie said and Jill watched in revulsion as she weaved the nasty worm around the hook.

"That has got to be one of the grossest things I've seen in awhile," Jill murmured.

"You never went fishing as a kid?"

Jill shook her head. "City girl."

"Ah. Well, my grandfather loved it. Whenever I'd go stay

117

with them, he'd take me out fishing. I was the only grandkid for the longest time so it was just me and him."

"Your boys?"

Carrie shook her head. "No. They never seemed to care for it. And part of that is James. When they were little, he never took the time to do things like that with them." She handed Jill the pole. "Now, just gently toss the line out."

"And if the yellow thing goes under, that's good, right?"

Carrie laughed. "Bobber. And yeah, that's good. Unless, of course, you're the fish," she added.

Jill sat quietly, patiently watching the bobber as it floated harmlessly on the water, part of her wishing the damn thing would go under so she could say she caught a fish. Of course the sane part of her prayed for no such thing. But a few minutes later when Carrie's bobber plunged under water, Jill stared excitedly as Carrie gripped the pole with both hands and lifted it up. Out of the water came what Jill assumed was a nice-sized fish, but before Carrie could get a net under it, the fish flipped in the air and dove back into the water.

"Oh, no," she said. "He was right there."

"Yeah. He was a good one too," Carrie said. Then she pointed at Jill's own line. "Look. See how it's moving? You probably have a perch or something nibbling at the worm."

Jill tensed, her grip tightening on the pole. "What does that mean?" But before Carrie could answer, her yellow bobber disappeared. "Oh my God!"

"Pull it up, pull it up," Carrie said as she stood beside her. "Easy."

But Jill jerked the line, sending her sprawling backward as the fish was flung over their heads and behind them. Carrie grabbed the line, holding the fish off the ground, a huge grin on her face.

"See? I told you you'd catch something."

Jill stared at the tiny fish then looked at Carrie. "Now what?"

Carrie moved the fish closer. "Now you take it off the hook."

Jill's eyes widened and she shook her head. "No way."

"But that's part of fishing, my dear. You catch something, you take it off the hook."

"Okay, not that I have anything against fish—I prefer them grilled—but I'm not touching that *slimy* little thing."

"And so you want me to?"

"Uh-huh," Jill nodded.

"You want to at least watch?"

"Nope."

But she did, staring as Carrie wrapped a hand around the fish to hold him still, then with the other hand, pulled and twisted the hook, trying to dislodge it.

"You're hurting him, aren't you?"

"I'll tell you what every fisherman would tell you. They don't feel a thing." Then she grinned. "I'm sure it hurts less than if you grilled him."

Finally the fish was free and Carrie dropped the line, walking slowly to the edge of the pier, kneeling down and gently placing the fish back in the water. Jill watched in fascination as the tiny fish flipped his tail and swam away.

"Oh, that was so sweet," she said seriously. "You didn't hurt him. That's why I love you—" she stopped, her eyes wide. She slowly shook her head. "I'm sorry. I didn't mean that like . . . well, I didn't mean—"

Carrie walked closer, her eyes pinning Jill.

"You love me?" she whispered.

Jill swallowed nervously, her mind racing. "I—I—"

Carrie tilted her head but said nothing, waiting.

Jill shrugged. "Is that what this is, Carrie?" Jill asked quietly. "Is this love?"

"We both know, don't we?" Carrie took her hands, holding them tight. "We're . . . we're connected somehow. It's beyond friendship, beyond this physical attraction we have. And Jill, it's so, so different than what we both have now. Isn't it?" She bent closer, lightly brushing Jill's lips with her own. "I can't explain it any more than you can." She took Jill's hand and placed it over her heart. "But I know it. I feel it."

"Yes." Jill closed her eyes briefly. "Yes, I feel it."

"Is it love?"

Jill nodded, her smile soft, sure. "Yes. Yes it is."

And she didn't hesitate the slightest bit when Carrie pulled on her hand, leading her up the walk and to the cottage. They both tugged at clothing, dropping it where they may. But it wasn't the bedroom Carrie pulled her into. It was the bathroom, with its bright red walls and huge walk-in shower.

"Gardening and fish," Carrie reminded her as she turned the water on full blast.

"Wouldn't have cared," Jill murmured as she pulled Carrie into the shower with her, wet skin sliding together as they embraced. Jill tasted the hint of wine on Carrie's tongue as she drew it into her mouth. Her hands wouldn't still as they moved across Carrie's skin, sliding along her spine to cup her buttocks and pull her flush against her. Carrie's hands, full of liquid soap, moved between them, lightly caressing Jill's breasts with soapy bubbles before moving lower. Jill's legs parted, an audible gasp left her when Carrie's fingers touched her. Their eyes held, fused together by a passion neither could explain. Jill's mouth opened as she struggled to draw breath, Carrie's fingers were relentless as they moved against her.

Jill's knees weakened and she braced herself, both arms spread out, holding herself upright against the shower walls as Carrie's mouth moved to her breast, her tongue hard against her nipple.

"I love when you do that," Jill whispered.

Carrie raised her head, her pale blue eyes dark with desire, her short salt-and-pepper hair damp from the spray. Her hands stilled, pulling away before grasping Jill's hips and turning her around. Carrie came up behind her, pressing hard against her buttocks as her hands reached around Jill to pull her firmly against her.

Jill moaned, feeling Carrie's breasts pressed against her back. Carrie's hands moved lower, spreading Jill's thighs again, her fingers moving leisurely through her wetness, brushing against her clit, causing Jill to groan deep in her throat. Her hips moved, rocking slowly, feeling the brush of Carrie's fingers as she pitched against her.

"Please," she whimpered.

Carrie bit down gently on her shoulder, her own hips rocking, moving in rhythm with Jill.

"Slowly," Carrie whispered into her ear.

And they did, their bodies moving as one, Jill arching forward to feel the delicious brush of Carrie's fingers against her hot center then back, meeting Carrie's thrust as Carrie ground against her. Slowly, slowly, then—as their breathing grew ragged—their motions increased, their hips working together, moving in unison, faster and faster, harder and harder until Jill was rocking back, loving the feel of Carrie as she pounded against her, loving the thrill of their dance, the tease of Carrie's fingers, the hot desire that shot through her with each stroke.

"Oh, *God*, Carrie . . . don't stop," Jill begged. "Don't stop, don't stop," she panted as their hips moved ferociously against each other. With eyes squeezed shut . . . that moment, that tiny moment between exhilaration and ecstasy, that one moment where everything stops . . . that moment held Jill suspended in time, stealing the breath from her, stealing the light from her eyes. That tiny moment seemed to last an eternity before releasing her, her breath expelled from deep in her gut, her body nearly convulsing as her orgasm echoed through her, touching her very soul.

When she thought she had nothing left to give, Carrie grasped her hips hard, pulling her forcibly back against her as Carrie sought her own release. Jill's fingers spread wide against the shower wall, supporting herself as Carrie thrust against her one last time before crying out Jill's name, then slumping heavily against her back as tremors shook her body.

"Oh, good God," Carrie murmured. "That was fantastic."

Jill slowly turned around to face Carrie, gathering her close again. They stood there, holding each other—recovering—long enough for the warm water to turn tepid. Only then did they move, pulling apart slowly, hands still touching, still stroking. Carrie reached around Jill to turn the water off then led Jill from the shower. They didn't bother with towels as they walked into the bedroom.

Carrie eased Jill to the bed and knelt before her, her hands moving slowly up her legs to her thighs, parting them. Jill watched, waiting, trembling the moment those hands spread her thighs.

"I love you," Carrie whispered. She looked up quickly, meeting Jill's eyes, holding them. "I love you."

The words echoed in Jill's brain as her eyes slid closed, Carrie's hot breath making it hard to speak, to think. She gave up her attempt at both when Carrie's arms wrapped around her legs, gathering her close, pulling her to her mouth. Jill's hands opened, her fingers gripping the sheets, trying to hold on as Carrie's tongue entered her. She moaned loudly when that same tongue circled her throbbing clit, teasing her nearly into oblivion until her mouth closed over her, suckling her, driving her to the edge in a matter of seconds.

Her hips arched, bucking uncontrollably as Carrie held on, her mouth never leaving her. Jill's scream came from deep in her throat, bursting out as she climaxed, and her legs squeezed together, trapping Carrie's head between her thighs, holding her there until the quaking in her limbs subsided.

She finally relaxed, lying limp on the bed. Her eyes flickered open, meeting Carrie's as she still lay between her legs. She attempted a weak smile but gave up.

"I think you've killed me," she murmured as her eyes slid

closed again. She heard Carrie chuckle, felt her move up the bed beside her but she still couldn't move.

"Come here," Carrie whispered as she pulled the covers back. "We'll nap for a bit."

"I should say no," Jill protested, but she crawled under the covers nonetheless. "I don't want to waste our time sleeping."

"Just for a little while," Carrie said, and she gathered her close, their naked bodies meeting under the covers, legs entwining.

"I love being with you," Jill whispered against Carrie's neck, her mouth moving sensually against her skin, her tongue coming out to tease before moving lower.

"I thought you were exhausted."

"Mmmm. Very," she said as her mouth continued its assault on Carrie's skin. When she brushed against Carrie's breast she heard her sharp intake of breath and her mouth closed around her nipple, her tongue twirling over the taut peak. She felt Carrie's hands move across her back, felt a hand snake into her hair and hold her tight against her breast. She looked up, finding Carrie watching her at her breast. Her heart swelled at the look in Carrie's eyes—desire, love.

She lifted her head slightly, inches away from Carrie's breast. The rise and fall of Carrie's chest brought her nipple close, then away. Jill's tongue came out, lightly touching, barely caressing the peak. She heard Carrie moan, felt Carrie's fingers dig into her back. She looked up again, Carrie's mouth was parted, her eyes dark, scarcely opened.

"I'm in love with you, Carrie," Jill whispered.

Carrie's eyes flickered open, a soft smile touching her mouth. Her hand moved through Jill's hair, touching her face, caressing her lips.

"Make love to me," Carrie murmured. "Will you make love to me?"

"Always," she whispered before again capturing Carrie's nipple in her mouth.

CHAPTER TWENTY-SIX

Jill watched Craig move silently about the kitchen, intentionally bypassing the chicken and mashed potatoes she'd picked up
at the fast food place in favor of a cold turkey sandwich. She
sipped from her tea as he meticulously lathered each slice of
bread with mayonnaise. She took a deep breath, wondering if the
silence was as uncomfortable to him as it was to her.

"How was the tournament?" Jill finally asked.

He shrugged. "Okay."

She nodded and raised her eyebrows. "And did you win?"

His laugh was sarcastic. "Oh, Jill, stop pretending like you
have an interest in our baseball team."

She started to protest but thought better of it. There was no
point in arguing the truth.

"Okay." She stood, tossing the rest of her tea down the sink
and rinsing out her glass. "I'm assuming your sandwich is not

just an appetizer. If you don't want any of this chicken, I'll put it up."

He laughed again. "Yeah, I know you went to a lot of trouble with dinner but this sandwich is just fine."

She gripped the countertop hard then spun around. "What the hell is wrong with you?"

"Oh, now that's a silly question, Jill."

She shook her head. "What do you want me to do?"

"I want you to be a goddamned wife, that's what I want," he yelled. He tossed his uneaten sandwich on the table and stormed from the room.

She leaned her head back, glancing to the ceiling with eyes closed, trying to hold on to just a tiny portion of the euphoric feeling she'd left with from Carrie's. But being back home— away from Carrie—it was hard to keep her spirit up, not when she was thrust smack into the middle of her rapidly unraveling life.

She took a deep breath, following after Craig as he ran up the stairs. She found him coming out of their bedroom with his pillow and a handful of clothes. She stopped, her eyes moving from the clothes to his face, his eyes angry as he looked back at her.

"What's left, Jill?" He shrugged. "This is it, isn't it? Me moving out of your bed?" Again, the sarcastic laugh. "We have a goddamned king-size bed and I haven't touched so much as your big toe in months. I don't see the point anymore."

She supposed he thought she would argue, would beg him not to move into the spare room but she looked at him with indifference. "As you wish," she said quietly.

He shook his head. "You're unbelievable. You can't even fight about it."

"Fight about what? You know how I feel. Do you think it suddenly changed overnight?"

He stared at her for a long moment. "What did you do

today?"

"What do you mean?" she asked, hoping her face did not reveal the inner turmoil she was feeling.

"You weren't home. What did you do all day?"

She didn't bother to ask how he knew this. Arlene had no doubt come by to check on her. "I was out and about," she said with as much casualness as she could muster. "Had errands, shopping."

His eyes narrowed. "You left before nine and didn't come home until after six," he stated, his tone accusing.

But she squared her shoulders. "There's really no need to have Arlene spy on me, Craig. It's certainly none of her business what I do on my own time."

"Fine. You want to continue this charade then so be it. Let me know when you're ready to tell me the truth."

He walked purposefully into the spare room, firmly closing the door behind him. She stared at the door for a moment, then turned, surprised to find Angie standing in the hallway. Their eyes met but Jill looked away, not knowing what to say to her daughter. She had most likely heard their entire conversation.

"Why don't you just get it over with?"

Jill walked down the stairs, ignoring her, hoping she would just go back into her room. But she followed Jill into the kitchen.

"What are you waiting for?" Angie asked.

"Angie, this is between me and your father. You don't know what's going on."

"I do know," she said loudly. "He's moved into the other room because you're having an affair," she accused.

"Angie, I'm not."

"Liar! Quit lying to me," she screamed. "You're seeing another man!"

"I'm not. I swear I'm not."

"You're lying! You're lying," she said again. "Why can't you just tell Daddy the truth? Just get it over with so I don't have to worry day after day what's going to happen."

"Angie, it's not that simple." She spread her hands. "And nothing's going to happen to you."

"Yes it is. You're going to get a divorce and make me leave here. You're going to move somewhere and make me go with you. Well, I don't want to go with you," she yelled. "I hate you! I want to stay with Daddy!"

She ran from the kitchen, her feet pounding on the stairs as she hurried back to her room. Jill heard the door slam and she hesitated, torn between comforting her daughter and her own fears. Carrie was right. If Angie found out about their relationship, it would ruin the fragile bond between mother and daughter. Angie would never understand, especially at her age.

She sank down heavily in the chair, staring at the half-eaten sandwich Craig had flung there earlier. She felt alienated. Even in her own kitchen, surrounded by familiar things, she felt little more than a stranger in her own home.

She leaned her elbows on the table, resting her chin on her hands as she stared across the room. Little by little, their accusations began to fade, being replaced by much more pleasant words, snippets of conversations between Carrie and herself, softly spoken words of love passing between them in their most fervent moments of passion, teasing words as they sat side by side at the pier, and then no words at all as they held hands by the flower garden, admiring their work as the clock slowly ticked the time away.

CHAPTER TWENTY-SEVEN

As soon as Jill walked into the cottage on Monday afternoon, she knew something was wrong. Carrie, who normally greeted her at the door, was at the pier, standing alone, staring out at the lake. Jill tossed her purse on the bar and made her way down the path, past the flower garden to the pier, her heels clicking on the wooden boards. Carrie turned at the sound, her eyes showing her surprise.

"Is it one already?"

"Yes." Jill tilted her head slightly, watching Carrie. "What's wrong?"

Carrie waved her hand dismissively. "Oh, nothing." She walked closer, wrapping her arms around Jill's waist and pulling her into a tight hug. "Saturday was fantastic and I missed you like crazy yesterday."

Jill smiled, pulling her head away to look at Carrie, then

bending closer, lightly kissing her on the mouth. "Yesterday was endless," Jill agreed. "In fact, this morning was endless." She pulled out of Carrie's embrace, watching her, trying to read her eyes. There was a wounded look there she'd never seen before. She took Carrie's hand and led her to their bench. "Now tell me what's wrong."

Carrie looked away. "Oh, it's nothing. Just a bad day yesterday."

"Then tell me about it. We've talked about everything. There aren't any secrets between us. Are there?"

"It's not that," Carrie said. She clutched her hands together as she stared at the lake. "It's just, yesterday morning, James . . . he confessed that he's been having an affair," she said quietly.

Jill's eyes widened. "Oh, God, I'm sorry." Then she frowned. "Is that the proper thing to say, given our circumstances?"

Carrie smiled slightly and shrugged. "I feel like an ass. I mean, here he was, so eaten up with guilt that he had to confess, and I just sat there, stunned."

"You didn't say anything?"

"We didn't have a screaming match, if that's what you mean. James and I have never been big fighters. It was all so calm and civilized. Of course, I don't know what my reaction would have been had I not been involved with you."

She stood, pacing, and Jill stayed quiet, waiting for Carrie to talk it out.

"She's the assistant manager at one of his stores," she said finally. Again a quiet laugh. "She's thirty-one. And good God, she's married too. I mean, what was he thinking?"

"So what did you say to him?"

"I asked him how long it had been going on," she said. "Since last fall." She turned and stared out over the lake. "Now I guess I know why he hasn't been concerned with our lack of a sex life." She turned back around. "God, that sounded just like the victimized wife, didn't it?"

"Well, it's a shock. I mean, you never suspected, did you?"

Carrie shook her head. "No. Of course I haven't really given anything a whole lot of thought lately." She sighed. "But that's not why I'm upset, Jill. I mean, how can I be upset with him for having an affair? No, I'm upset with myself. I had the perfect opportunity to tell him about you, about us. Yet I didn't." She walked back to the bench and sat down again. "And like a typical wife, I let him wallow in his guilt, let him beg for forgiveness, let him plead with me not to tell the boys. And all the while I'm thinking what an ass I am."

Jill linked arms with her. "But why did he tell you? Does he want to be with this woman?"

Carrie shook her head. "No. Like I said, she's married, has kids. It was just something that happened."

"And is still happening?"

"No. And I think that was why the guilt got to him." She sighed. "He said he thought maybe I was having my own affair and that was why I didn't miss him being around."

"Oh."

"I still couldn't tell him. If I'd told him, then everything would have focused on me and it would be like his little affair just went away, because mine is a bit bigger, seeing as how you're a woman and all," she said with a hint of a laugh. Then she buried her head in her hands. "What a mess," she muttered.

Jill leaned closer and bumped her shoulder. "Well, speaking of messes, Craig has officially moved into the spare room."

Carrie looked up. "It's gone that far?"

"And Angie confronted me. She has informed me that she hates me and if we get a divorce she wants to stay with Craig."

"Oh no."

Jill shrugged. "She's fourteen. She's supposed to hate her mother."

"And Craig?"

Jill sighed. "I don't know." She turned, looking at Carrie,

falling into her eyes. "What are we going to do?"

"I won't lie, Jill. I've thought of us being together. How wonderful it would be to go to sleep with you at night, to hold each other, to wake together to greet a new day. How wonderful would that be?" She turned, her eyes moving across the water. "But this is so foreign to us both." She laughed. "We don't exactly have experience at being lesbians."

Jill laughed too, slipping her arm around Carrie's shoulders and following her gaze out over the water.

"But I worry about you," Carrie continued. "You and Angie. If she left your life, if she could never forgive you, would you eventually grow to resent me, resent *us*?" she asked quietly. "And is what we have worth you losing a child?"

Jill nodded, her eyes slipping closed. "In other words, you don't know what we're going to do either."

Carrie turned, her eyes softening as she saw the love Jill didn't try to hide. She leaned closer, her kiss feather-light. "I don't have a clue," she whispered.

CHAPTER TWENTY-EIGHT

"Feel like going to the park?" Carrie asked one warm, sunny day weeks later.

Jill laughed. "You miss the ducks?"

Carrie held up a loaf of bread, her eyes smiling. "I have an urge."

Jill walked closer, her arms sliding around Carrie's waist. "An urge, huh?" She pulled them together, loving the familiarity of their embrace, loving the gentle kiss they shared. "I would love to go to the park with you."

"Wonderful. And just so you don't starve, I made us sandwiches to take along."

Jill pulled away, seeing the paper sack on the bar. She nodded and smiled. "Just like old times."

"Do you mind?"

"Of course not." She reached for the sack. "It'll be fun." Or so she thought until she saw the crowded parking lot minutes later. She groaned loudly. "Good God. Half the town's here."

Carrie laughed. "School's out. What'd you expect?"

"I guess I'd forgotten what it was like during the summer." She discreetly reached across the console and rubbed Carrie's thigh. "And I've gotten spoiled with our own private part of the lake."

"I know." Carrie drove through the parking lot, looking for a spot. She found one toward the end and pulled in. She sat there, hands still on the wheel. "Maybe this wasn't such a good idea."

"Oh, it'll be fine. We'll take the trail through the woods to the piers. It'll be less crowded."

And it was. They met only a handful of joggers and two teenagers on bikes. For Jill, it was one of those days—those warm, sunny days—when she wished she didn't have a job to rush back to. How nice would it be to spend the afternoon with Carrie?

"I know exactly what you're thinking," Carrie said.

"Oh, do you?" Jill countered, playfully bumping her with her shoulder.

"Wanna play hooky this afternoon?"

Jill laughed. "Okay. You got me."

"You know, you've got some clothes at the cottage. Shorts and stuff," she said with a shrug. "Maybe you could?"

"Oh, Carrie, I wish I could. But I've got payroll due. I can't put it off."

"Probably just as well. If we start that, I'll be asking you at least once a week to blow off work."

"I know." Jill turned, wishing they had the luxury of holding hands. "It's just that an hour a day is not nearly enough."

"You know, we haven't had a Saturday in a while," Carrie reminded her.

"No, we haven't. And I don't know when we can."

"Has anything changed at home?"

"Other than Craig has volunteered to teach summer school, which is a first for him." Jill sighed. "It's his attempt at being the martyr, because you know, there's nothing at home for him." She stopped. "And Angie barely speaks to me."

"I'm sorry."

"No. I can't blame her. I can't blame Craig for what he's doing either. I mean, our wedding anniversary is this week. How awkward is that going to be?" She touched Carrie's arm briefly, then started walking again. "I've come to the realization that I'm holding him hostage," she admitted. "Regardless of what happens with us, it's not fair to him."

"You want to divorce him?"

"They don't have to find out about us, Carrie. That doesn't have to be the issue."

"It'll come up, you know it. Eventually it will."

"Then I'll deal with it. I just don't want it to affect you."

Carrie was silent as they walked on, the trail coming to an end near the piers. Most of the paddleboats and canoes had been rented and kids and adults alike laughed and played out on the lake. Carrie paused, finding the flock of ducks that had taken refuge in a tiny cove not far from the piers. She pointed and Jill nodded, following her through the trees.

"I didn't tell you, but Josh asked me point-blank if I was seeing someone," Carrie said.

"When?"

"Last week. He said he could tell something was up between me and his dad."

"What did you say?"

Carrie looked away, out to the lake. "I told him I wasn't," she said quietly. "But Jill, I came so close to telling him the truth." She turned, watching Jill. "Josh is such a great kid. And I think he would understand about this, about us. I really do." She opened the loaf of bread, handing Jill several slices. "But then I didn't want to burden him with the weight of all this. He's going to be going off to college in a couple of months. I don't want him worrying about me."

As they walked closer to the water, the ducks saw them and swam closer, some getting out of the water to clamor at their feet. They silently tore apart the bread and tossed it to the dozen or more ducks that gathered around them. Grandma Duck joined them, limping noticeably as she fought for her share of bread.

"What are we going to do?" Jill finally asked.

"I don't know," Carrie said as she bent down to hand Grandma Duck a piece of bread. She glanced up, meeting Jill's eyes. "I just know I love you. That's all."

Jill's breath caught as it always did when Carrie uttered those words to her. Yes, that was all. Love. But a love neither of them quite knew what to do with. Jill stood back, watching the ducks, watching Carrie. Carrie finally stood, her eyes squeezing shut in a grimace.

"What's wrong?" Jill asked.

"It's nothing," she said as she rubbed her temples. "Just have a killer headache. Comes and goes." She gave a brief smile. "You want to find a park bench?"

Jill shook her head. "I'd rather go back to the cottage and have a little alone time."

Carrie glanced at her watch. "Fifteen minutes."

Jill took her arm and led her back down the trail. "I can be a few minutes late."

CHAPTER TWENTY-NINE

Harriet knocked once then cracked the door, sticking her head inside. Jill looked away from her monitor, eyebrows raised.

"What's up?"

"You have a visitor," Harriet whispered.

Jill frowned. "Who?"

"It's your mother-in-law."

"Oh, God," Jill said with a groan. "You have *got* to be kidding me."

"Sorry."

"What does she want?" Jill whispered.

"She just asked to see you."

Jill stood. "Okay, okay." She smoothed her skirt then walked to the door. Harriet had disappeared and Jill forced a smile as she greeted Arlene.

"What a surprise, Arlene. Is something wrong?"

"Of course not. Can't I visit my daughter-in-law?"

"You don't normally." Jill stood back, motioning to her office. "Come in."

Arlene took a seat in one of the visitor's chairs, her eyes moving around the room, landing on the few personal items Jill kept there. She saw the disapproving look on her face and knew what was coming. There were no pictures of Craig in her office. In fact, the only one of Angie was taken nearly five years ago.

"It's so impersonal here, Jill. I would have thought you'd have more reminders of your family. You seem to have forgotten you have one."

"Listen, Arlene, if you came here to discuss my marriage, you should have saved yourself the trip. It's none of your business."

"I did not come here to discuss *your* marriage. I came to discuss my son's."

"Then perhaps you should discuss it with him."

Arlene smiled smugly. "Oh, I have dear. And it's positively horrendous what you're doing to him. Making him sleep in the spare bedroom as if you are little more than roommates. And poor Angie, you've ruined her for life, I'll have you know. That child is in tears nearly every day."

Jill stood abruptly. "I'm not going to sit here and listen to this, Arlene." She pointed to the door. "Good-bye."

But Arlene made no attempt to leave.

"Eighteen years of marriage and you're not even willing to fight for it? What kind of a woman are you? I never imagined you to be so heartless, Jill."

"Get out of my office, Arlene."

"If you don't love him, then divorce him, let him go so he can get on with his life. He's still young. He can still find someone who can treat him with the dignity and respect he deserves."

Jill leaned forward, her hands on the desk. "You have no idea what it was like to live with him, Arlene. I was invisible in my own house. How would you like to be married to a man who was never around? To a man who hadn't matured past twenty-one? It got old."

Arlene shook her head. "That's his job. And if you'd bothered to keep your teaching job all those years ago, you could have spent more time together. But no, you wouldn't listen to me. Well, I hope you're happy now. You've ruined your husband's life, your daughter's life." She stood quickly, her purse grasped tightly in her hands. "At least have the decency to tell him the truth." She spun on her heels and was gone before Jill could reply.

"Unbelievable."

And when Harriet stuck her head in the door a short time later, Jill was still standing, still staring into space.

"Need to talk about it?"

Jill looked at her for a long moment then sighed. She and Harriet were eight-to-five friends, nothing more. They rarely discussed their home life. And she didn't think now was a good time to start.

"I'm sorry, but I overheard," Harriet said.

Jill moved back to her chair, finally motioning for Harriet to sit. Telling someone she was having marital problems was one thing. Telling them she was having an affair with a married woman was quite another matter altogether.

"Craig's her only child," Jill said by way of explanation.

"Well, I've noticed you haven't really been yourself lately."

Jill laughed. "That's an understatement." She folded her hands in front of her, idly twisting the wedding band she still wore. "I guess you could say Craig and I are separated," she said.

"Oh my goodness. I had no idea."

"We're still living in the same house, he's just moved into the spare room. And it's beyond awkward," she admitted.

"Are you going to divorce?"

Jill looked up and met her eyes. It was a decision she wrestled with daily. She knew the answer, of course. She just hadn't been able to say it. But now she nodded.

"Yes. I'm going to file for divorce."

"I'm so sorry. I know with a child, it must be very difficult."

"What's more difficult is realizing your child wants to stay with her father, not you." Jill leaned back in her chair, turning her head to look out the window. "It's very complicated, Harriet."

"I know it's none of my business but is there someone else?"

She wanted so badly to tell her. The love she felt for Carrie was nearly bursting at the seams and she just wanted to tell someone about it, tell someone how happy she was, how fulfilled she was when she was with Carrie. But she couldn't. Not yet.

"I just told my mother-in-law it was none of her business." She smiled to soften her words. "I should tell you the same thing."

"Of course. I understand."

As she moved to go, Jill stopped her.

"Harriet? I appreciate the offer to talk. Really I do."

Harriet just nodded and slipped from the room.

"I mean it, Craig. You've got to talk to her. She's not our goddamned marriage counselor," Jill said as she slammed the cabinet door.

"What? I'm to forbid her to talk to you?"

"That would be a start." She added the pasta to the boiling water, aware of Craig watching her. "Where is Angie?"

"She's at my mother's."

"Great. Another chance for Arlene to brainwash her."

"She's just worried about her. And I'm sure Angie tells her stuff."

Jill turned. "You mean more than you tell her?"

"I'm sorry but I just need someone to talk to sometimes."

"But your *mother*?"

"Why not her? We're close." He looked at the bottle of wine on the counter. "You want me to pour you a glass?"

"Please." Jill stirred the spaghetti sauce, wondering at Craig's civility this evening. Especially regarding the wine. "And I'm just saying, there are some things mothers don't need to know. Our sex life being at the top of the list."

Craig actually laughed and Jill realized it was the most conversation they'd had in months. And she admitted it was much better than the silence they'd been living with.

"You know, the Fourth is coming up," he said as he placed the glass of wine within her reach.

"Yeah. And?"

"Well, we usually have a get-together here, with the group," he said.

"You mean your softball buddies?"

"And their wives. You act like I only invite my friends."

"They are your friends, Craig. But I get along with most of the wives, yes."

"Well, do you want to do it this year?"

Jill put the spoon down and turned, watching him. *Was he serious?*

"You want to have a party? Here? Wouldn't that be a little awkward?"

"Yeah. You're probably right. I just thought . . . well, I thought we could do something normal, you know. Like we used to."

Jill turned back to the stove, hating the blanket of guilt that was slowly, slowly settling over her. Yes, they always had a party on the Fourth of July. Her birthday was the fifth so it was a double celebration. Arlene baked a cake and they would sing "Happy Birthday" to her. Then at dusk, pile into cars to go watch the fireworks out at the lake.

The lake. *Their* lake. She wondered if Carrie and her family went out there too.

"So what do you say?"

She sighed. "Okay, fine. If that's what you want to do."

"Thanks, babe."

She turned back around. "Craig, this doesn't change anything."

He nodded. "Oh, I know. I just think it would be good for us, for Angie, to do something familiar. She's really having a hard time, Jill."

"So I hear. She doesn't exactly speak to me," she said as she drained the pasta. "Take the bread out of the oven, would you?"

"You ready for me to call Angie home?"

"Yes, everything's ready."

And it was. Spaghetti and meatballs. Garlic bread with an obscene amount of cheese melted on top. And a healthy salad that Craig and Angie would no doubt lather in dressing. She sighed again. How dysfunctional was this evening? She'd come home pissed off, still steaming about Arlene's visit, and Craig had been attempting to cook dinner. Again, guilt hit, so she took over for him, browning the meatballs before he could ruin them and finding some homemade spaghetti sauce in the freezer instead of the jar he had by the stove. And here they were, about to sit down to a family meal together. She and her husband—who were living in separate bedrooms—and her daughter, who had barely said more than ten words to her in the last few weeks.

And now you've agreed to a birthday party.

She filled her wineglass again, hardly noticing the slamming of the door as Angie walked past.

CHAPTER THIRTY

A tiny round cake, laden with what Jill assumed were forty candles—all burning hotly—greeted her when she got to the cottage. She laughed then pulled Carrie into a quick hug.

"How did you know?"

"I snuck a peek at your driver's license. I know it's only the third but I wanted to do it before the holiday."

"How sweet of you," she said with a kiss. "But I'm not sure I'm supposed to be enjoying forty quite this much."

"Nonsense. Forty is a great year."

"I happen to agree with you." Jill bent down, blowing out all forty candles at once. She clapped excitedly then hugged Carrie again. "I love you."

She felt Carrie's arm pull her tighter, heard the quiet sigh Carrie uttered when their bodies pressed together.

"I love you too. Happy birthday."

The quiet, gentle kisses turned to more as their bodies moved sensually against each other. After all this time, Jill was still surprised how her body reacted to Carrie's touch.

"I have champagne," Carrie murmured into her ear.

"Later," Jill whispered, turning her head to capture Carrie's mouth. "Make love to me first," she breathed against her lips. She felt Carrie tremble at her request and her eyes slid closed when Carrie's tongue wrapped around her own.

No more words were spoken as Carrie led her into the bedroom, carefully removing her clothes. Jill lost patience as she stepped out of her skirt then reached for Carrie's shorts, sliding them down Carrie's hips in one motion.

"In a hurry?" Carrie teased.

"As a matter of fact, yes."

Jill laid down on the bed, pulling Carrie with her, her thighs spreading to allow Carrie to settle between them. But as soon as Carrie's bare skin touched her own, Jill rolled them over, pinning Carrie beneath her.

"I changed my mind," she whispered before her mouth closed over Carrie's breast.

"I won't complain," Carrie murmured, and Jill smiled as she moved lower, wetting a path across Carrie's stomach before cupping her hips and pulling her to her waiting mouth.

CHAPTER THIRTY-ONE

As soon as Jill heard Craig whistling in the kitchen as he piled ground beef into the bowl, she knew the party was a mistake. It would serve no purpose other than to give him false hope that their marriage was salvageable. And it wasn't. But when she pushed open the swinging door to the kitchen and found him there, a baseball cap turned backward on his head, packages of wieners mingled with the ground beef on the counter, she didn't have the heart to say anything. She decided she could play along for a day.

"You're starting early," she said as she reached for the coffee pot.

"Well, I didn't want you to have to mess with all this." He grinned. "Of course, if you could do your special seasonings thing with the burgers, that'd be great."

She touched his arm. "I tell you what, why don't you go set up the volleyball net and I'll tend to this."

"You don't mind?"

She smiled. "I believe this has always been my job."

"Great. Because I've still got to run to the store and get cokes and stuff."

"Would you like me to make a pitcher of tea?"

"Oh, don't go to any trouble. You know all the guys will bring beer."

"I remember. But I think your mother prefers iced tea."

Craig stopped, his eyebrows raised. "You're worried about my mother? Are you okay?"

Jill laughed. "I just don't want her to have anything to complain about."

"She'll complain that your spicy burgers are too spicy, as always," he said before closing the door.

"Yes, as always," she muttered to herself as she assembled the seasonings. And as much as Craig was making this little party out to be no big deal, she was actually terrified of it. There would be questions, she had no doubt. Her absence at the softball games this summer surely raised some eyebrows. And if not that, she doubted seriously that Arlene had been able to keep their marriage problems to herself.

But questions . . . she wasn't ready to answer any. Would she just pretend everything was fine between her and Craig, just to avoid questions? She shook her head. That would only confuse Craig, Angie . . . and her in-laws. And that was the last thing she wanted to do.

"I don't want to go to the party."

Jill stared at her daughter, both of them standing with hands on their hips. She cocked her head, her frown as pronounced as Angie's. "You don't have a choice."

Angie stomped one foot, then crossed her arms at her waist.

"I should have a choice. I'm not a child! And anyway, I've been invited to Shelly's."

"Look, I don't want to go to this party any more than you do. But he's making me. So if I've got to go, you've got to go."

Angie stared at her. "Are we going to the lake for fireworks?"

"I suppose so. We always do."

Angie shifted her feet then finally uncrossed her arms. "Can I invite Shelly over here?"

Jill smiled. "Of course. You can invite whomever you like."

They stared at each other for a moment before Angie spoke. "Okay. Well, I might hang around then."

"Good. I'd hate to think you were going to run away from home on the Fourth of July."

Angie smiled. "Well, it is your birthday."

Jill sighed. "Yeah. I'm forty."

"Good God! Forty? Man, you're *old*," she said as she fled from the room.

Jill watched the swinging of the kitchen door, a smile on her face. "My daughter is teasing with me," she murmured. "Whatever in the world is wrong with her?"

"Who are you talking to?"

Jill turned, finding Craig in the doorway, his cap still turned backward. Her eyes widened. "Oh my God. You shaved your moustache."

He laughed. "You'd make a terrible detective. It's been gone all week."

"But you've had it forever. You had it when we met. Why in the world would you shave it?"

He rubbed his upper lip with his fingers, smiling. "I figured I needed a change."

"Well, not that my opinion holds a lot of weight anymore but please grow it back. You look naked without it."

He grinned. "How would you know? You haven't seen me naked in months."

Before she could respond, he was gone, his whistling echoing through the house as he headed upstairs.

"Well, I see you've come to your senses."

Jill lowered her glass of wine. "How so?"

"Or is it just because it's your birthday you agreed to this party?" Arlene waltzed into the kitchen, a huge cake in her hands. "And isn't it a bit early for wine? You don't want to have the guests talking, do you?"

Jill blew out her breath, vowing not to let her mother-in-law get to her today. So she smiled sweetly. "As with everything else, Arlene, it's none of your goddamn business." She had the pleasure of seeing her mother-in-law gasp before walking out to the deck. Craig and his father were measuring off the out-of-bounds lines for the volleyball games. Despite her loathing for her mother-in-law, she'd always gotten along well with Carl. But given the current situation, she wouldn't blame him if he chose to ignore her. He didn't.

"Jill, how are you?"

"Fine, Carl, thanks."

"I'm glad you both decided to have the party. It just wouldn't seem like the Fourth without it."

Jill looked at Craig, nodding at his smile. "So I'm told." She walked out into the yard to join them. "Your mother made a cake," she said. Then, quieter, "You don't suppose she would resort to arsenic, do you?"

Craig laughed. "I'll eat the first piece."

Jill bypassed the lawn chairs Craig had set out on the deck, choosing instead the more familiar swing. Craig was certainly in a good mood today. So was Angie, for that matter. She wondered if it was only the prospect of the party, or if they thought—since she'd agreed to it—that things were going to return to normal.

She pushed off with her foot, setting the swing in motion,

watching them as they marked the lines. Their guests would be here any minute and she still wasn't sure how she was going to play it. Pretend everything was fine, just to avoid uncomfortable questions? In other words, lie. Or be herself and keep her distance from Craig, letting everyone know that the rumors they'd most likely heard were true. Or perhaps she could use her current favorite line—*none of your goddamn business.*

She smiled, imagining saying that to Whitney Myers, wife of Craig's best friend. Wife, teetotaler and Sunday school teacher. Of all of Craig's friends' wives, she got along well enough with most of them. However, she and Whitney had never hit it off. She always came away with the impression that Whitney was judging her. And finding Jill sorely lacking.

She stood in the shadows of the deck, watching the others as they laughed, their conversations free and easy. With each other, at least. But with her, the conversations had been guarded, forced. She took a deep breath and swirled the wine in her glass, wondering if she dared to open a second bottle.

"Jill?"

She turned, surprised to find Mindy standing behind her, watching. She straightened, moving away from the pillar she'd been leaning against.

"Hey, Mindy," she said. Then she found her manners. "Are you enjoying yourself?"

"Great party. As always."

"Thanks."

Mindy moved closer, blocking Jill's view of the backyard. Jill assumed she was to have her first inquisition.

"I know we haven't been the best of friends but if you need someone to talk to, I'm here for you."

Jill raised her eyebrows. "Why would I need someone to talk to?"

"Well . . . you and Craig, I mean, it's no secret you guys are having problems," she said quietly. "We haven't seen you two out together in ages."

Jill bit her lip, just barely holding back her new favorite response. Instead, she smiled and lightly touched Mindy's arm.

"Thanks for your concern, Mindy, but I'm fine. Really."

"So you and Craig, you're not . . . well, you're not separating?"

It's none of your goddamn business.

Again she smiled. "Our personal life . . . well, it's personal. You understand."

"Okay, then." She stepped away. "Good. Well, again, if you need to talk," she said.

"Thanks. I appreciate it."

But her easy smile vanished as soon as Mindy walked away. These people—these women—who she had called friends, weren't really, she realized. They were just acquaintances she saw sporadically at games and on the rare occasions they shared a meal. And Mindy's offer as a confidant now was based more on curiosity than concern.

And with that revelation came another. She did indeed need to open the second bottle of wine.

"The burgers were great, babe."

Jill flicked her eyes at him, cringing at the endearment she'd grown to detest. "Thanks."

"But you're not really having a good time, are you?"

She smiled. "Why? Can you tell I'm sitting here, praying I get teleported to Hawaii or something?"

"That bad?"

"Craig, I know you want some normalcy in your life but having this party didn't change anything," she said softly. "I'm sorry."

He shrugged. "Angie had a good time. I haven't seen her this happy in months."

Jill nodded. "I know. And I realize how this is wearing on her. I really do." She took a deep breath. "Maybe it's time we made some decisions instead of continuing like we are," she said gently.

She saw him swallow, saw his eyes close and she truly felt sorry for him.

"You mean like divorce?" he finally asked.

She nodded but he shook his head.

"I'm not ready to talk about that, Jill. Can we just not talk about that now?"

She nodded again. "Okay, Craig."

He stood. "Do you still want to go to the fireworks?"

"I think I'll bow out, if you don't mind."

He shoved his hands in the pockets of his shorts, his eyes hinting at his inner turmoil. "Sure. I understand. I'll take Angie and her friends then run them home afterward." He motioned to the yard. "Don't worry about all this. I'll clean it up in the morning."

She nodded and forced herself up, forced herself to go through the motions of telling everyone good-bye, and she graciously accepted the words of thanks that were tossed her way as their guests left. And in a matter of minutes, quiet prevailed and she was left alone. Even Arlene left without a parting comment. No doubt she was still smarting from their earlier conversation.

Now alone, Jill went about the task of cleaning up the kitchen and putting away the leftovers. And despite Craig's directive about the backyard, Jill tidied the deck enough so that she could sit in the swing.

And think.

Her wine had been replaced by a bottle of water and she slipped off her sandals, sitting barefoot as she put the swing in motion. Darkness had chased the light from the sky and she knew the fireworks would soon follow. Even now, sporadic bursts could be heard in the distance.

She relaxed for the first time all day, letting the motion of the swing soothe her. Her earlier consumption of wine had mellowed her mood to nearly the point of contentment. So finally, at last, she allowed her thoughts free rein, allowed visions of Carrie to form, to grow . . . to consume her.

Any doubts that lingered about their relationship were dispelled today. Even though she and Craig were able to function somewhat normally together, were able to talk and tease even, didn't change the fact that she was in love with someone else.

And how it came to be that she could find herself so totally in love with another woman, she didn't have clue. She only knew her heart belonged to Carrie. Not Craig.

With that, she accepted the inevitable.

She would file for divorce.

CHAPTER THIRTY-TWO

After the long three-day weekend, Jill was in more of a hurry than usual to get to the cottage. She closed the gate behind her as she drove down the driveway, glad she'd worn a sleeveless blouse with her slacks today. It was sunny and hot but even then, she'd prefer to have lunch in the shade of the garden rather than inside.

But Carrie was nowhere to be found when she got out. She looked down to the pier but it was empty. So was the tiny table they'd placed under the trees by the flower garden.

She knocked once on the sunporch door then went inside. The interior door to the cottage was closed and she assumed Carrie had the air conditioning on today.

"Carrie?" she called as she stuck her head inside.

"Here."

Carrie was sitting in the dark, her head leaned back on the

loveseat.

"What's wrong?" Jill asked, walking closer and rubbing her shoulder.

"I'm all right."

But when she looked at Jill, her eyes were filled with pain.

"Are you feeling ill?"

Carrie closed her eyes. "I've had this damn migraine all weekend. Nothing I take seems to help."

Jill sat down beside her, touching her face. "You feel warm. Do you think you have a fever?"

Carrie took her hand and squeezed and pulled it to her. "I'll be fine now that you're here."

"Well, I don't have a lot of experience with migraines but I do know you're supposed to be in a dark, quiet room." She stood, pulling Carrie up. "Come on. Lie down in the bedroom. I'll make a cold compress for your head."

"Will you stay with me?"

"Of course. Come on."

Jill pulled the covers back and helped Carrie remove the shorts she was struggling with. After closing all the blinds, she untied the drapes, letting them fall to keep out even more light. Then she soaked two hand towels in cold water. One, she put in the freezer for future use, the other, she placed across Carrie's forehead.

"That feels good," Carrie murmured.

Jill crawled in beside her, sitting up against the pillows and lightly rubbing Carrie's head. She smiled as Carrie moaned and continued her ministrations, pressing harder around Carrie's temples, trying to ease her pain.

"You know, you've been complaining of headaches a lot lately," Jill commented. "Is that unusual for you?"

Carrie opened her eyes briefly then shut them again. "Just allergies," she said. "Some years are worse than others."

Jill leaned down and kissed the top of her head, then settled back against the pillows again, her fingers continuing to massage Carrie's scalp. Before long, Carrie's even breathing signaled that she had fallen asleep. Jill watched her, noting the frown that marred her features, even in sleep.

Finally, as the clock ticked nearer to two, Jill eased out of bed. In the kitchen, she got the cold compress out of the freezer and returned to the bedroom. Carrie had shifted, rolling to her side as if searching for Jill. She took the wet cloth from her head, replacing it with the one from the freezer. Carrie moaned once but didn't wake. Jill kissed her lightly on the cheek then moved away. As an afterthought, she took Carrie's cell phone from her purse and turned it on, then placed it beside the bed. She would call her later, just to make sure she didn't sleep the afternoon away.

"I love you," she whispered as she kissed her cheek one last time before leaving.

But she didn't even make it back to the office before her own cell rang.

"I woke up and you were gone."

"I was hoping to sneak away quietly so you could sleep longer," she said.

Carrie chuckled. "Who could sleep with an ice cube on their head? But I feel better. I guess your cold compress helped."

"Good."

"I'm sorry I messed up our lunch."

"You didn't mess it up. We were together."

Carrie paused. "How was the party?"

"Oh, it was . . . it was tolerable. No, that's not even the right word. I survived it, I guess I should say. But I almost felt like I wasn't really there, you know? Like my body was there but I wasn't. Like I no longer belonged there."

"Is that how you feel? Like you don't belong there?"

"Yes, that's how I feel." She cleared her throat, thinking this conversation should be had in person and not over the phone but she didn't want to wait any longer. "Carrie, I'm going to file for divorce."

Carrie was silent for only a moment before Jill heard her take a deep breath. "Jill, I want us to be together. If you're serious about doing that, then I want us to be together."

Jill slowed as she turned into the parking lot. She stopped and turned off the car, her hand gripping the phone tightly.

"Are you sure?" she asked.

"Yes. I'm prepared for whatever fallout there may be. I'm not concerned about James, just my boys. But sweetheart, are you prepared? Have you really thought all this out? Angie? Your family?"

"I can't go on like this, Carrie. I just can't."

"Okay. Okay." She sighed and Jill thought she heard the tiniest of moans.

"Headache back?"

"Yeah. We'll talk about this tomorrow. I think I'm just going to lie down for a little longer."

"Good. Do you want me to give you a wake-up call later?"

"That'd be nice. I love you, Jill," she murmured before disconnecting.

CHAPTER THIRTY-THREE

"Where the hell did this come from?" Jill said out loud as the downpour began. Out the window of her car, she saw the dark clouds gathering to the north and she turned her wipers on faster. She would be soaked. Her umbrella was hanging on the coatrack in her office. They hadn't seen rain in weeks.

She was thankful for the remote Carrie had given her for the gate as she pushed the button, waiting for it to open before driving through. She pushed it again, closing the gate behind her and driving on through the rain. But at the cottage, she was surprised to find the driveway empty.

Dodging water puddles as she ran along the path, she hurried into the sunporch and out of the rain. Inside, it was dark and quiet, no sign that Carrie had been there yet today. She pulled her cell phone out, debating whether to call her or not. She thought better of it, in case Carrie was someplace where she couldn't talk.

She busied herself with lunch, foregoing their normal fare of sandwiches when she found soup in the pantry. But as the clock ticked closer to one thirty, she began to worry. Again, she picked up her phone, but again, she decided against calling.

And only moments later she heard Carrie's van, heard the door slam. She walked into the sunroom, waiting. Carrie rounded the corner, their eyes meeting through the windows. Jill knew immediately that something was wrong.

"Sorry I'm late," Carrie said. She moved into Jill's arms and Jill pulled her close.

"What's wrong?"

"I was at the doctor," she said.

"What do you mean?"

"Oh, you know, these damn headaches I've been having."

Jill took her arm and led her into the cottage, easing her down on a bar stool. "Have they been worse?" she asked as she ran her fingers through her damp hair.

"Unbearable lately."

"Why didn't you tell me?"

Carrie shook her head. "I didn't want you to worry. They did a ton of tests. I've been there all morning. They did a CAT-scan too. But the symptoms are like a damn sinus headache," she said as she rubbed her forehead.

"When will you know something?"

"Probably not until Monday." She wrapped her arm around Jill's waist and pulled her closer. "But don't worry, okay. It's probably just my allergies in overdrive."

But Jill did worry. Try as she may, Carrie couldn't hide the pain in her eyes. And for the first time, Jill realized how thin Carrie was getting. The last week or so, she hadn't had an appetite at lunch, only picking at her food.

"Feel like soup?"

Carrie shook her head. "I've been poked on and stuck with

needles," she said. "I think I'll pass. But you go ahead and eat."

Jill leaned closer, her lips caressing Carrie's temple, then moving across her cheek before finding her lips.

"I love you."

Carrie turned on the chair, her legs opening as she pulled Jill between them, holding her close. "I love you too. So much," she murmured.

Jill smoothed her hair, her fingers gliding through the short locks, now more salt than pepper. Another thing Jill had just noticed. She closed her eyes, pulling Carrie to her breast, feeling Carrie burrow there.

"Is there anything I can do?" she whispered.

Carrie squeezed her tight. "No, no. I'm just so tired."

"Then come on," Jill said, pulling away and helping Carrie to her feet. "I'll help you into bed."

"It's probably time for you to go already, isn't it?"

"Just about. But it's okay. You can rest. I'll leave the soup out. You need to eat something, Carrie. It'll make you feel better."

"Sure. Okay. Leave the soup out," she said, her words slow, deliberate.

Jill stopped, her eyes searching Carrie's. "Maybe I should stay with you."

"No, it's okay. They gave me something for the headache. It's probably kicking in."

"Are you sure?"

"Yes. Sure."

Jill pulled back the covers on the bed, then slowly undressed Carrie as she sat mutely on the edge. She paused, her hand cupping Carrie's cheek.

"Are you sure you're okay?"

Carrie closed her eyes. "I'm fine, love."

CHAPTER THIRTY-FOUR

Jill held up the sack when she walked into the cabin. "I picked up burgers. You feel like eating out in the garden?"

Carrie shook her head, her eyes moving around the room quickly, then settling back on Jill.

"Please don't say you're not hungry," Jill said as she walked closer. "Getting you to eat something lately has become a full-time job." She set the bag on the bar then wrapped her arms around Carrie, smiling when she heard her sigh.

"I love you, Jill."

Her brief kiss became lingering, and Jill closed her eyes, falling into Carrie's embrace. But Carrie stopped, pulling away.

"We need to talk, Jill," she said quietly.

Five simple words, yet Jill felt her world crumbling. Their eyes fixed on each other, holding, searching. Jill's breath left her and she shook her head.

"No," she whispered.

"Yes." Carrie took her hand and led her into the sunroom. "Let's sit."

Jill shook her head. "No. I don't want to sit."

Carrie sighed wearily. "Please? I need you to do this for me."

"Oh, God," she whispered. "You're sick, aren't you?"

Carrie nodded. "Yes." She patted the seat beside her. "Come."

Jill took a deep breath then sat down, her eyes searching Carrie's. "How bad?"

Carrie took her hand and brought it to her lips. "Bad. It's bad, Jill."

"Oh, God. Your headaches?"

Carrie nodded. "They found . . . they found tumors, Jill."

Jill stared, unable to breathe, unable to look away. "No." She shook her head. "No."

"I've been thinking. You know, it's not too late. You can stay with Craig, you can try to salvage your marriage."

"No! No, no, no," she said loudly. "I don't want him! I don't want my marriage! I just want you."

Carrie looked away. "I'm sorry."

"Oh, God, Carrie. I'm sorry," she said around her tears. "I'm sorry." She drew Carrie to her, her lips moving without thought before burying her face against Carrie.

"I love you so much," Carrie whispered. "I'm sorry."

"No." Jill cleared her throat then pulled away. "We'll get through this." She took a deep breath and wiped at her tears. "So . . . what do they say? The doctors . . . what do we do?"

Carrie shook her head. "You don't understand. There's nothing to do."

Jill's eyes widened. "What do you mean? No treatment?"

"No. They're inoperable, Jill."

Her words sunk in and Jill slowly shook her head. "No," she whispered. "No. I won't let you give up."

Carrie took her hand again, holding it tight. "I'm not giving up. There's nothing to give up, Jill. There is no chance."

"There are treatments. There are always treatments."

"No. No, I won't go through that. And for what? To prolong this for another month at the most? No. I don't want my last days on this earth to be in a hospital, hooked to machines, stuck with needles . . . sick as a dog. No! I won't do it."

Jill stood, moving away from her, her eyes wide. "I call that giving up."

Carrie closed her eyes, shaking her head. "No, darling. It's just accepting reality, that's all." She stood, slowly walked across the room to Jill. She took her hands again. "There's not much time left," she said softly. "I know it. I can *feel* it. Don't make me go through chemo." She shook her head again, finally giving in to the tears Jill knew she had been hiding. "Don't make me do that for you."

Jill broke down then, her sobs shaking her whole body, and she clung to Carrie, taking comfort, trying to give comfort.

"No, baby, no. Don't cry," Carrie murmured. "This won't help anything. Don't cry," she said again. "Your tears are too valuable to lose."

"Don't leave me."

"It's not up to me."

"But—"

"No. No," she whispered, her lips lightly brushing Jill's mouth. "Please stop crying. Please? I can't bear to see you like this."

"I'm sorry," Jill said, her tears still falling.

"We don't have much time, Jill. Not much time at all."

"Oh, God." Jill wiped at her eyes, trying to get herself under control and failing. "I'm sorry."

"No. I'm sorry." She tried to smile. "I don't suppose there's ever a good time or place to tell someone news like this." She took a deep breath. "I'll have to tell them tonight."

Them meant her family and the reality of their situation—of their relationship—hit home. This was what they had. One hour each day. Even now, during this time of sorrow and angst, that's all they would have. One hour. Her tears fell anew.

"I know, darling. I know," Carrie murmured. "As much as I want to spend my last hours with you, we both know I can't. I'll be with my kids instead. But know my thoughts will be of you. My last thoughts will be of you."

"No, no, no," Jill whispered.

"Please don't be sad. Look at me, Jill." Jill raised her face, ignoring the tears that flowed freely down her cheeks. "Our souls, they're connected. We'll be together again. Just like before. Just like now, in this life. There'll be others."

"I so want to believe you."

Carrie wiped at Jill's tears then brought their mouths together.

"Then believe."

CHAPTER THIRTY-FIVE

"You want to talk about it?"

Jill turned, startled. She shook her head, putting the swing in motion again, but he walked closer anyway.

"I ordered a pizza for dinner," he said.

Jill cleared her throat. "I didn't feel like cooking." She knew her voice was still hoarse from crying but she didn't care. She didn't care about anything right now.

"Are you going to tell me what's wrong?"

She sighed. "It's nothing." *God, it was everything.*

"You've been out here all evening." He walked out of the shadows, the moon casting the only light. "You've been crying."

She closed her eyes. "Please, Craig. I just want to be alone."

"Is it something I've done? Something I haven't done?"

"Craig, it has nothing to do with you, with us." He stood there with his hands in the pockets of his shorts, still watching her. "Really. I just want to be alone."

"Okay. Well, I'll let you know when the pizza is here."

"Fine."

She leaned back in the swing, her eyes closed, wishing—hoping—for a different outcome to the day. She was beyond numb, beyond drained, beyond . . . empty.

They'd taken the afternoon, after she had called in to Harriet. There were questions but none that Jill could answer. She'd simply told Harriet to shut down her computer and lock her office. And then she'd hung up and the tears came again. So they walked to the pier and sat. Just sat. They didn't talk much. They sat, they touched, they cried.

And at five, Carrie had gathered her close, had told her good-bye. Her eyes had been filled with pain, pain she'd tried to hide from Jill.

"I'll see you tomorrow?"

Carrie nodded. "Sure. Same as always."

Jill had driven away, her eyes glancing again and again into the rearview mirror, seeing Carrie standing on the driveway, watching her. The feeling that she would never see Carrie again was like an ominous premonition, one she tried to dispel as she drove away.

But now, sitting here in the dark—alone—that feeling came to her again. Much like all those months ago when she'd first met Carrie, when she felt their meeting was preordained, their affair inevitable. Much like that, she knew deep in her soul that she would never see Carrie again.

And again, the tears came.

CHAPTER THIRTY-SIX

She'd thought . . . maybe . . . Carrie's van would be there. But she wasn't really surprised to find the driveway empty. Because she *knew*.

She was surprised, however, to see the roses on their table in the sunroom. Roses and a bottle of wine. Her breath caught and she covered her mouth, trying so hard not to cry at the sight of the lone wineglass.

"Oh, Carrie."

She stood at the door for the longest time, gathering herself, her eyes moving over the table, seeing the papers, seeing the note. She finally moved, walking closer, instinctively bending to smell the flowers.

"Why did you do this?" she whispered.

But the note drew her and she sat down, her eyes glancing at the words, reading them quickly before her vision became blurry with tears.

I won't make this long. You don't need that and I'm not sure I could manage it. There are just some things you need to know. First, the cottage. It's as much yours as mine. And it didn't become a home to me until you came into my life. So I've transferred the title to your name. All you need to do is sign the paperwork I've left for you. My attorney's card is there. I've given him all of your information. He'll be in contact with you. Also, there's a bank account that I opened in your name. It's not a huge sum, Jill, but it was mine and I wanted you to have it, not James. It was the money from Joshua and from his land.

I know how hard this is for you. I came into your life and turned your world upside down, and now I'm leaving you. But it doesn't hurt so much, Jill, knowing we'll be together in another life, another time. As brief as it was, I couldn't have loved you more even if we'd had twenty years together.

Please don't cry for me. I'll be with you. You just have to look for me. I've asked for my ashes to be spread at the park, near the pier, where you and I walked and talked, where we fed the ducks . . . where we met.

There was another sentence or two, but Jill couldn't go on. She cried out then with one swing of her arm, she knocked the roses and wine to the floor, glass shattering on the tile from her fit of grief. There amongst the mess stood the lone wineglass, undisturbed by her fury.

CHAPTER THIRTY-SEVEN

Present Day

Jill shifted on the bench, her gaze sliding from the old woman back to the countless headstones that dotted the landscape. "And just like that . . . she was gone." Jill dabbed at her eyes, her tissue in shreds and she dug in her purse for another one. "I never saw her again. And three weeks later, I read the news . . . in the paper," she said, tears again falling. "So quick. I'm in shock still, I think. There wasn't time to say good-bye. There wasn't time to say all the things I wanted to say, needed to say. She was just gone." Jill paused for breath, just now noticing the lengthening shadows as the sun slipped from the sky. She'd been talking for hours. "I'm so sorry, I've just been rambling on."

The old woman took her hand and squeezed, her own eyes misting with tears. "Not rambling, dear. You've been telling me of a great love. Thank you for sharing that with me."

Jill blew her nose then cleared her throat. "Yes. We fell in love. People do that, you know," she said, almost apologetically. "And when you're falling in love, you believe in things so strongly." She paused, tears again welling in her eyes. "And I believe. I truly do. Is that crazy? Is it crazy to believe—to *hope*—that there's another lifetime that we'll be together? Do you think about that with your Eddie?"

She shook her head. "No. The Bible says it's not so. But I believe I'll see Eddie again. In heaven. Not in another lifetime." She patted her hand. "But I've learned through the years that everyone has different beliefs." She leaned closer. "That doesn't make it wrong."

Jill was silent for a moment, absently rubbing at her eyes, knowing she must look frightful. She finally turned. "No one knows. No one. Just you." She touched her heart. "A love so strong inside of me and no one knows."

"And you crashed the service today just to see them, to put faces to names?"

"Yes. Is that awful of me? I thought maybe I might feel . . . well, might feel her here."

"From what you've told me, it's not here you'll find her. You have the cottage now. That's where she'll be."

Jill laughed bitterly. "Yes. I have the cottage. A place I can't bear to go to, yet a place I'll never be able to part with."

"Nonsense. You'll go there because that's where she is. That's where you'll find your peace." She pointed to the grave. "That's why I come here. To me, this is where Eddie is, this is where I put him. That's what I was taught to believe." She stared at the grave, her wrinkled face hinting at a smile. "Oh, I feel his presence in the house, always will I suppose. But he's here. And I have my bench where I can come and talk to him. It eases the pain somewhat." She surprised Jill by putting a thin arm around her shoulders and pulling Jill closer. "Death . . . it's so hard to be the one left behind," she said quietly. "But we go on. That's what we do." She pulled away. "Now, you go on home. You've got some decisions to make."

Jill nodded, then leaned over and kissed the wrinkled face. "Thank you," she whispered. "Thank you for . . . well, just thank you."

Jill squeezed her shoulder one last time, then walked away, surprised by the lessening of the pain in her heart.

"If you ever need to talk, you know where I'll be," she called to Jill.

Jill turned, watching as Bea's glance slid back to the grave, back to her Eddie.

CHAPTER THIRTY-EIGHT

She gave herself a week. A week to get her emotions under control, a week to make sure there weren't any complications with the cottage and a week to feel confident about her decision.

Despite everything that had happened to her in the last year, her decision to leave Craig really had very little to do with Carrie. She'd been unhappy in her marriage long before Carrie came into her life. But still, divorce was something she'd never even considered before.

So she waited for Craig to get home, determined to tell him, determined to get on with her life. She couldn't continue this any longer. Between his constant questions and her fits of tears, the last few weeks had been a challenge for both of them. But it was time to give them both some relief. So she waited, sitting quietly out on the deck, the familiarity of it a comfort as she put the swing in motion. He would be home soon, she knew. And

Angie, with the new school year barely a month old, had fallen into her old habit of going to Arlene's afterward until they called her home.

Then she heard it, the garage door opening, the truck door slamming. She closed her eyes for a moment, trying to gather her courage. She didn't want to hurt Craig but what she needed to tell him would hurt him deeply. After everything that had transpired between them—their fights, their silence—Craig still thought they could resurrect their marriage.

"Hey. Thought you'd be out here."

She nodded, waiting for him to join her.

"I thought, when you said you wanted to talk . . . well, I thought maybe it would be a good thing," he said. "But it's not, is it?"

"No, Craig." She took a deep breath. "We can't do this any longer."

"But—"

"No, please. Let me finish." She cleared her throat before continuing. "It's been a tough year for you, I know. But I've got to do this, Craig. I'm going to file for divorce," she said quietly. "It's best for everyone, Craig."

He walked away, his steps echoing on the deck as he paced back and forth. Then he asked the question Jill knew he would ask.

"You've always denied it but there's another man, isn't there? Just tell me."

She stared at him, her eyes filling with tears she didn't try to hide. "No, Craig. There was never another man."

"Then why? Why would you want to divorce?"

"Because I have nothing to offer you anymore. Nothing. And it's not fair to you to go on like this, Craig. I can't stay and be your wife." She looked away, then back at him, meeting his eyes. "I'm sorry, but I'm just not in love with you. And you need someone who is. You need to find someone who loves sports as much as you do. Then she'll go to all your games, she'll stand up and cheer for you, she'll love you for that part of you. But I can't be that person. I'm *not* that person."

"I don't understand." He paced again. "What does that mean? You want me to move out?"

She shook her head. "No. This is your home. This is Angie's home."

"Angie? You want Angie to stay with me?"

"Yes. Your mother is close by." She smiled sadly. "Angie doesn't want to be with me, Craig. Besides, I wouldn't be very good for her right now. So we'll work out some arrangement. I just want what's best for her."

He leaned his head back and stared at the sky, then let out his breath. "I guess I shouldn't be so surprised. It's been so long since it's been normal." He turned and looked at her. "Where will you go?"

"Actually, I've got my eye on this . . . this cute little cottage out at the lake." She wiped at the tears sneaking down her cheek. "I think it'll be perfect for me."

CHAPTER THIRTY-NINE

Despite her initial apprehension about the cottage, she found she actually felt at peace there. And she came across many pleasant surprises as she sorted through Carrie's things. Namely, a painting that Carrie had tucked into the bedroom closet, complete with gift-wrapping and a card. The wrapping paper indicated it was to be for Christmas but Jill couldn't wait.

And when she tore the paper off, she slid to the floor beside it, her tears flowing freely. The painting, in watercolors, was of her, sitting by the pier on their bench, the greenness of the trees and the blueness of the water depicting a spectacular early summer day. And beside the bench was the huge pot they'd bought and stuffed full of blooming red and yellow flowers.

"Thank you," she whispered.

The painting exemplified their entire summer. Carefree days filled with love, filled with colors and flowers, filled with gentle conversation and even gentler touches.

She took a deep breath, then looked at the painting again, this time without tears. This time with wonder as she remembered the woman who had painted it. The woman who showed her the meaning of true, genuine love.

It was weeks later—with the air hinting at fall and a light rain falling—she was standing in the sunroom, staring at the lake and the pier, when she felt a pull, a familiar urging to go outside. She tilted her head, her eyebrows drawn together in a frown. This feeling, this unexplained inclination, turned into a yearning as her feet finally moved, carrying her silently to the door. And just as the first time she'd met Carrie, it was like a hunger that guided her. She didn't question it. She walked out, ignoring the rain, just following the silent command of her heart.

The water was still, only the tiny droplets of rain disturbing the smooth surface. And she stood there, looking out over the lake, searching for what, she didn't know. And then she saw them off in the distance.

Ducks. A dozen or more.

They swam purposefully toward her, their quiet clamors carrying across the water. She watched, aware that her heart was beating quickly, her breath hissing between her lips. Then, out of the pack she came, wings flapping strongly, her gray head a dull contrast to the brightly colored mallards around her.

Jill dropped to her knees as Grandma Duck ran across the water, away from the flock before settling down again. Her sobs came quickly and her chest ached as she knelt there, waiting for the duck to swim closer. So overwhelming was the feeling of Carrie's presence, she stopped breathing, simply staring out over the water, waiting—believing.

And just as quickly as her sobs came, laughter bubbled out unexpectedly. She sat on her heels, tears still running down her cheeks as she laughed in the rain.

"Oh, God, Carrie . . . I should have known you'd come back to me as that damn duck."

Publications from
BELLA BOOKS, INC.
The best in contemporary lesbian fiction

P.O. Box 10543, Tallahassee, FL 32302
Phone: 800-729-4992
www.bellabooks.com

OUT OF THE FIRE by Beth Moore. Author Ann Covington feels at the top of the world when told her book is being made into a movie. Then in walks Casey Duncan the actress who is playing the lead in her movie. Will Casey turn Ann's world upside down?
1-59493-088-0 $13.95

STAKE THROUGH THE HEART: NEW EXPLOITS OF TWILIGHT LES-BIANS by Karin Kallmaker, Julia Watts, Barbara Johnson and Therese Szymanski. The playful quartet that penned the acclaimed *Once Upon A Dyke* are dimming the lights for journeys into worlds of breathless seduction.
1-59493-071-6 $15.95

THE HOUSE ON SANDSTONE by KG MacGregor. Carly Griffin returns home to Leland and finds that her old high school friend Justine is awakening more than just old memories.
1-59493-076-7 $13.95

WILD NIGHTS: MOSTLY TRUE STORIES OF WOMEN LOVING WOMEN edited by Therese Szymanski. 264 pp. Twenty-three new stories from today's hottest erotic writers are sure to give you your wildest night ever!
1-59493-069-4 $15.95

COYOTE SKY by Gerri Hill. 248 pp. Sheriff Lee Foxx is trying to cope with the real-ization that she has fallen in love for the first time. And fallen for author Kate Winters, who is technically unavailable. Will Lee fight to keep Kate in Coyote?
1-59493-065-1 $13.95

VOICES OF THE HEART by Frankie J. Jones. 264 pp. A series of events force Erin to swear off love as she tries to break away from the woman of her dreams. Will Erin ever find the key to her future happiness?
1-59493-068-6 $13.95

SHELTER FROM THE STORM by Peggy J. Herring. 296 pp. A story about family and getting reacquainted with one's past that shows that sometimes you don't appreci-ate what you have until you almost lose it.
1-59493-064-3 $13.95

WRITING MY LOVE by Claire McNab. 192 pp. Romance writer Vonny Smith believes she will be able to woo her editor Diana through her writing . . .
1-59493-063-5 $13.95

PAID IN FULL by Ann Roberts. 200 pp. Ari Adams will need to choose between the debts of the past and the promise of a happy future.
1-59493-059-7 $13.95

ROMANCING THE ZONE by Kenna White. 272 pp. Liz's world begins to crumble when a secret from her past returns to Ashton . . . 1-59493-060-0 $13.95

SIGN ON THE LINE by Jaime Clevenger. 204 pp. Alexis Getty, a flirtatious delivery driver is committed to finding the rightful owner of a mysterious package. 1-59493-052-X $13.95

END OF WATCH by Clare Baxter. 256 pp. LAPD Lieutenant L.A Franco Frank follows the lone clue down the unlit steps of memory to a final, unthinkable resolution. 1-59493-064-4 $13.95

BEHIND THE PINE CURTAIN by Gerri Hill. 280 pp. Jacqueline returns home after her father's death and comes face-to-face with her first crush. 1-59493-057-0 $13.95

18TH & CASTRO by Karin Kallmaker. 200 pp. First-time couplings and couples who know how to mix lust and love make 18th & Castro the hottest address in the city by the bay. 1-59493-066-X $13.95

JUST THIS ONCE by KG MacGregor. 200 pp. Mindful of the obligations back home that she must honor, Wynne Connelly struggles to resist the fascination and allure that a particular woman she meets on her business trip represents. 1-59493-087-2 $13.95

ANTICIPATION by Terri Breneman. 240 pp. Two women struggle to remain professional as they work together to find a serial killer. 1-59493-055-4 $13.95

OBSESSION by Jackie Calhoun. 240 pp. Lindsey's life is turned upside down when Sarah comes into the family nursery in search of perennials. 1-59493-058-9 $13.95

BENEATH THE WILLOW by Kenna White. 240 pp. A torch that still burns brightly even after twenty-five years threatens to consume two childhood friends. 1-59493-053-8 $13.95

SISTER LOST, SISTER FOUND by Jeanne G'fellers. 224 pp. The highly anticipated sequel to *No Sister of Mine*. 1-59493-056-2 $13.95

THE WEEKEND VISITOR by Jessica Thomas. 240 pp. In this latest Alex Peres mystery, Alex is asked to investigate an assault on a local woman but finds that her client may have more secrets than she lets on. 1-59493-054-6 $13.95

THE KILLING ROOM by Gerri Hill. 392 pp. How can two women forget and go their separate ways? 1-59493-050-3 $12.95

PASSIONATE KISSES by Megan Carter. 240 pp. Will two old friends run from love? 1-59493-051-1 $12.95

ALWAYS AND FOREVER by Lyn Denison. 224 pp. The girl next door turns Shannon's world upside down. 1-59493-049-X $12.95

BACK TALK by Saxon Bennett. 200 pp. Can a talk show host find love after heartbreak? 1-59493-028-7 $12.95

THE PERFECT VALENTINE: EROTIC LESBIAN VALENTINE STORIES edited by Barbara Johnson and Therese Szymanski—from Bella After Dark. 328 pp. Stories from the hottest writers around. 1-59493-061-9 $14.95

MURDER AT RANDOM by Claire McNab. 200 pp. The Sixth Denise Cleever Thriller. Denise realizes the fate of thousands is in her hands. 1-59493-047-3 $12.95

THE TIDES OF PASSION by Diana Tremain Braund. 240 pp. Will Susan be able to hold it all together and find the one woman who touches her soul?
1-59493-048-1 $12.95

JUST LIKE THAT by Karin Kallmaker. 240 pp. Disliking each other—and everything they stand for—even before they meet, Toni and Syrah find feelings can change, just like that.   1-59493-025-2 $12.95

WHEN FIRST WE PRACTICE by Therese Szymanski. 200 pp. Brett and Allie are once again caught in the middle of murder and intrigue.   1-59493-045-7 $12.95

REUNION by Jane Frances. 240 pp. Cathy Braithwaite seems to have it all: good looks, money and a thriving accounting practice . . .   1-59493-046-5 $12.95

BELL, BOOK & DYKE: NEW EXPLOITS OF MAGICAL LESBIANS by Kallmaker, Watts, Johnson and Szymanski. 360 pp. Reluctant witches, tempting spells and skyclad beauties—delve into the mysteries of love, lust and power in this quartet of novellas.   1-59493-023-6 $14.95

ARTIST'S DREAM by Gerri Hill. 320 pp. When Cassie meets Luke Winston, she can no longer deny her attraction to women . . .   1-59493-042-2 $12.95

NO EVIDENCE by Nancy Sanra. 240 pp. Private Investigator Tally McGinnis once again returns to the horror-filled world of a serial killer.   1-59493-043-04 $12.95

WHEN LOVE FINDS A HOME by Megan Carter. 280 pp. What will it take for Anna and Rona to find their way back to each other again?   1-59493-041-4 $12.95

MEMORIES TO DIE FOR by Adrian Gold. 240 pp. Rachel attempts to avoid her attraction to the charms of Anna Sigurdson . . .   1-59493-038-4 $12.95

SILENT HEART by Claire McNab. 280 pp. Exotic lesbian romance.
1-59493-044-9 $12.95

MIDNIGHT RAIN by Peggy J. Herring. 240 pp. Bridget McBee is determined to find the woman who saved her life.   1-59493-021-X $12.95

THE MISSING PAGE A Brenda Strange Mystery by Patty G. Henderson. 240 pp. Brenda investigates her client's murder . . .   1-59493-004-X $12.95

WHISPERS ON THE WIND by Frankie J. Jones. 240 pp. Dixon thinks she and her best friend, Elizabeth Colter, would make the perfect couple . . .   1-59493-037-6 $12.95

CALL OF THE DARK: EROTIC LESBIAN TALES OF THE SUPERNATURAL edited by Therese Szymanski—from Bella After Dark. 320 pp.
1-59493-040-6 $14.95

A TIME TO CAST AWAY A Helen Black Mystery by Pat Welch. 240 pp. Helen stops by Alice's apartment—only to find the woman dead . . .   1-59493-036-8 $12.95

DESERT OF THE HEART by Jane Rule. 224 pp. The book that launched the most popular lesbian movie of all time is back.   1-1-59493-035-X $12.95

THE NEXT WORLD by Ursula Steck. 240 pp. Anna's friend Mido is threatened and eventually disappears . . .   1-59493-024-4 $12.95